Books by Ron Glick:

Godslayer Cycle
One
Two
Three *(July, 2015)*

Chaos Rising
Tarinel's Song
Immortal's Discord

Oz – Wonderland
The Wizard In Wonderland
Dorothy Through the Looking Glass
The Wonderful Alice of Oz

Trivia Books
Ron El's Comic Book Trivia Volume 1
Ron El's Comic Book Trivia Volume 2
Ron El's Comic Book Trivia Volume 3
Ron El's Comic Book Trivia Volume 4
Ron El's Comic Book Trivia Volume 5
Ron El's Comic Book Trivia Volume 6
Ron El's Comic Book Trivia Volume 7
Ron El's Comic Book Trivia Volume 8
Ron El's Comic Book Trivia Volume 9
Ron El's Comic Book Trivia Volume 10
Ron El's Comic Book Trivia Volume 11
Ron El's Comic Book Trivia Volume 12
Ron El's Comic Book Trivia Volume 13 *(January, 2015)*

The Oz-Wonderland Series

Book III

The Wonderful Alice of Oz

by

Ron Glick

ISBN-13: 978-1505561517 - ISBN-10: 1505561515

To Megan Lynn

The light in the darkness that sparked this story.
Herein lies the conclusion, but not the end.

Table of Contents

Chapter 1

The White Rabbit's Revolt

"Oh dear," muttered the White Rabbit, his hands twisting feverishly. "Oh dear, oh dear, oh my."

Not for the first time, the Rabbit glanced over the hedge to look upon the scene there. As was so common with the King and Queen, things were ever changing and to look away for a moment would mean to lose one's place, after all. He barely kept up with things when he was away serving the Crown in his other duties, much less when he was present and overseeing the changes personally.

The King and Queen – though to be honest, the Rabbit could not be sure if the Hare was still the Queen or not, as the King now wore both the crown *and* the queen's gown – were involved in a game of croquet, much as the Queen of Hearts herself often engaged in. But since the King did not have the equipment for the game, he had taken to playing with whomever or whatever lay about the yard in front of the King of Hearts' home. Presently, that included a dozen court attendees, a fair handful of tea cups, and what the Rabbit presumed to be the Dormouse himself rolled into a ball when he was not running and dodging the players who were all trying to kick the poor little thing with their feet.

As the Rabbit looked on, the Dormouse recovered from his latest booting and managed to get his feet under him enough to make a run for it. Unfortunately for the mouse – or perhaps purposefully, as it was so hard to tell such things – the Dormouse was headed directly for the King. However, just before the Dormouse could collide with the King, the regent yanked up his dress and extended his legs as far as they would go, forming a giant ring through which the Dormouse could flee.

"Score!" cried the Hare.

"Score!" echoed the rest of the people and animals standing or leaning about the yard. Most were arranged in either self-formed hoops through which the Dormouse-ball could be knocked, though there were a few standing about the fringes who would dart after the mouse whenever he would manage to get enough of his senses back to attempt to run away from the game.

"Foul!" cried the King, throwing his dress down in a fit. "That hoop was not there a moment ago!"

"Was so!" cried the Hare, bounding over to the King. "You were just hiding it beneath your gown."

"Hmmm," mumbled the King. "I must say, I think we need a rule about that."

"Well, you *are* the King," said the Hare. "Make one."

"One what?" asked the King, his face notably befuddled.

"A rule," prompted the Hare.

"What kind of rule?" asked the King.

"About hidden hoops, of course."

"Can we hide hoops?"

"We can if there's a rule!"

"Hmmm," mumbled the King again. "Perhaps we should make a rule about making a rule?"

"Your majesty," grunted one of the animals serving as a hoop – a weasel, if the Rabbit were not mistaken. The Rabbit was amazed at how the creature could gather air in his lungs to speak at all bent over backwards as he was. "We already have a rule about making rules."

"We do?" chimed in the King and Hare together.

"Indeed," gasped the weasel-hoop. "Rule 7 and 3/4: 'The King makes all the rules.' You made it yourself."

"I did?" marveled the King, splaying his hand across his chest in a self-aggrandizing fashion. "Why, you must show me this rule! Is it a big one?"

"How could it be?" asked the Hare. "All rules are only as long as the ruler they belong to, and rulers are always the same length – the size of your foot."

"Who ever made *that* rule?" asked the King.

"The King of Hearts did," piped up the Weasel again. "Rule 12: 'The King's foot shall be the measurement of all things.'"

"Well, the King of Hearts is not here," said the Hare, stiffening. "He abdicated and the Hatter is King, and that is that."

"I do so agree, Hare," nodded the King enthusiastically. "I should truly make you my queen again."

"Oh pish," said the Hare, covering his face with one hand while waving his other at the King daintily. "You will flatter me all over again."

"I think you are flat enough, my dear Hare." The King shook his head vigorously. "But I shall make you my queen regardless. Here, take this dress from me. All it's good for is hiding hoops, at any rate, and there is no rule about that."

At this, the White Rabbit once more ducked behind the shrub to begin his pacing again. "Oh dear, oh dear, oh dear," he grumbled. "It is all that Mile High Girl's fault. The Dorothy one, not the Alice one. Though I dare say that Alice would not have been much better. They both have not a brain between them!"

The Rabbit reached instinctively for his breast pocket where he kept his watch as he had done so often. The timepiece was almost a security blanket for the nervous creature, giving him a constant sense of rigidness in an otherwise insane world. Time was ever constant, after all – or so he told himself. Even if he always arrived late no matter how much time his pocket watch told him there was, he was convinced that it was the one constant upon which he could rely.

However, as he reached for his watch, his hand once more clanked against the rigid metal of the breastplate he wore. Times of war required one to dress the part, and in his case, he had chosen to wear the traditional armor that his station required. Even if it was ever so cumbersome in following any kind of regimented routine. His spectacles were forever out of reach in his inner pouch, and most annoyingly, he could not reach his breast pocket to check his timepiece.

The Rabbit shook his hand in frustration. "And the Giant's, of course," he added to his earlier list of people with whom to place blame. "He started this war, after all. If it were not for him, why, I would never have had to send for the Mile High Girl and get the wrong one in the first place!"

Once more, the Rabbit began pacing, worrying his hands vigorously. "And the King would not have discovered that I was working for the King. Or for the Queen of Hearts, for that matter."

The white creature stopped in mid-pace and stood up rigidly, though no one was actually around to witness his posturing. "I serve the Crown," he insisted pompously. "How can I serve the Crown if I do not serve all who wear it?"

Ever since the civil war began, the White Rabbit had been run ragged with his hustling and bustling. The Queen of Hearts had called for the King of Hearts' head, and that had started the war. But then the King of Hearts cast off his crown and set off in search of the Giant who had turned his Queen against him. The Hatter then came along and donned the crown himself (for what was a crown, if not another fancy hat?), which made him the King, as well. With two Kings and at least one Queen (depending on who was wearing the Hare's gown at any given moment), this left the Rabbit in the service of three monarchs, and it was his duty by oath to serve each and all of them.

For the Queen of Hearts, his duties were to seek out the King of Hearts. For the King of Hearts, it was to aid him in finding the Giant. For the Hatter-King, it was... well, to do whatever the Hatter-King wanted at any given moment. And that changed frequently, which made the Hatter-King the most time-consuming of the three to serve. It also required the Rabbit to attend the Hatter-King's court more than any of the others.

In spite of how demanding his work had become of late, the Rabbit had juggled it all with a the pomp and flourish for which he had earned such a trusted position before the Crown. Yet in serving the King who was once known only as the Mad Hatter, he accepted the one duty that had led to his current crisis – he had sent Bill the Lizard above to retrieve the Mile High Girl, who insisted her name was Alice.

Once before, the Mile High Girl had come to the King and Queen's court and testified in a trial, though when she had first attended, she did not appear to be a mile high, at all. In fact, she was quite a normal sized girl at the start. But as the trial proceeded, the girl had begun to grow, earning her the name with which she would thereafter be known. In fact, she grew so very tall that she simply grew up and out of sight entirely.

The Queen of Hearts had ordered the Mile High Girl forever banished thereafter, and only an order of the Crown could have rescinded that command. And this was precisely what the Hatter-King had done.

"Why, if someone that tall can hide, it can only be because no one is tall enough to see him", had reasoned the Hatter-King. *"So have someone who is just as tall to do the searching! Who do we know who is at least that tall?"*

Of course, the only ever-so-tall person anyone could recall was, in fact, the Mile High Girl who had been banished by the Queen. But, since he now wore the crown, the Hatter cared not at all for the rules of the Queen.

The White Rabbit closed his eyes and took a deep breath. "If only *I* had gone instead of Bill," he sighed. "Then perhaps this *other* Mile High Girl would not be running about causing so much trouble!"

All had been fine enough when Dorothy had first answered Bill's call. She had come to meet the Hatter-King and been respectful enough, even if she did have a tendency to babble nonsense which all around her were constantly forced to correct. She confessed to knowing the Giant by another name, but that did not seem as catastrophic a conundrum as the Rabbit had feared. And she had left on her search for the Giant in the end, which was precisely what she had been brought to do. It was only when she actually *found* the Giant herself that things had come undone.

The Rabbit had left the Hatter-King's court to go spend some time in service to the King of Hearts in his search for the Giant. After all, the King needed to know that the Rabbit had seen to it that a plan was afoot to find the Giant with the help of the Mile High Girl. And, sure enough, armed with the knowledge that instead of searching for the Giant, they could instead search for the Mile High Girl was all that was needed to track the girl to the Giant himself.

When confronted, however, the Mile High Girl began to babble her nonsense again. She actually *told* the King of Hearts that the White Rabbit was still working for the Queen of Hearts *and* was also working for the new King who had taken up the King of Heart's crown. The Rabbit had tried to teach the girl that it was not proper to tell one King that someone was working for *another* King, but would the girl listen? Of course not. And so she had blabbered on and on and before one knew how to stop her, she had announced that the Rabbit was working for several monarchs, not just the King of Hearts.

The King did not take to the information well, at all, But instead of demanding the girl's head on the end of his lance, the King actually turned on the Rabbit. On *him!* The King of Hearts had actually called the Rabbit a *traitor!* How could he be a traitor when, above all others, he had remained completely loyal to the crown in *spite* of a war between them? Why, he should have been given a medal – instead, he had been chased off at the point of a sword by one of the very Kings that he served.

"A traitor," grumbled the Rabbit. "Me, a traitor. Why, the Mile High Girl is the traitor, not me. And the Giant. Him, too. They are the ones who won't follow the rules!"

Yet therein lay the crux of the Rabbit's dilemma. He had been named a traitor by the Crown, yet he was still in service to the Crown. At least, he still served two who wore crowns, and they *expected* him to continue to do so. But he was also an enemy of the Crown, as declared by the King of Hearts. He could not possibly be both a servant *and* an enemy of the Crown. And yet... he was.

The Rabbit paused in his internal debate, and stretched high to look over the hedge once more. By now, the Hare was again in the queen's gown. He was also perched atop one of the court attendants who was bent over acting as a hoop, attempting to use the dress to hide the woman upon which he sat. Unfortunately, the dress was not large enough to extend all the way to the ground from where he sat.

"I honestly do not see how you made it look so easy," said the Hare. "I cannot get this hoop hidden at all."

"We made the rule, Hare," responded the King. "You will have to find a way to hide the hoop if you wish to use it."

The Rabbit plopped upon the ground. At least his presence was not being called for just yet. This gave him a small margin of time – though without his watch, it was anyone's guess as to how much time that would actually be. The sound of his hand hitting the metal reminded the Rabbit once more of how unavailable that resource was to him.

"To be a traitor, or not to be a traitor," mused the Rabbit. And he would have mused further if his thoughtful musings were not suddenly interrupted by the small figure of the Dormouse bursting through the hedge and colliding directly into the back of the Rabbit's armor.

The Rabbit looked down befuddled as the tiny creature shook its head vigorously. "The stars," the mouse peeped. "Could you please stop the stars?"

"Oh, buck up," scolded the Rabbit. "You haven't the problems I have. All you must do is run from feet. I must run to *and* from them."

The Dormouse looked up at the other creature seated beside him. "Oh, Mr. Rabbit," his high pitched voice squeaked. "I am ever so sorry for knocking you over. I have never done that to anyone before. And to be honest, I didn't know I could."

"It is quite alright," said the Rabbit. "You did not knock me down further than I already was."

"Oh, that's good. I would hate to be known for doing anything new. Someone might find it useful, what with the war and all." The mouse let out a loud yawn. "Bad enough that I have not been able to nap all day. The King decided to play a game, and I was an important part, it seems. Truly hard to sleep when you are, you know." -

The Dormouse lay upon the ground and curled into a ball. "But now that I am away..." The mouse barely finished before a high whistle sound could be heard escaping his mouth.

"Oh, don't be doing that just yet," said the rabbit, poking at the mouse until he raised his head. "I could use a set of ears to listen, as my own are quite worn out on this subject."

The Dormouse opened and closed his mouth sleepily, squinting up at the Rabbit. "I assure you, it shall only be for the barest of moments..." Once more, the mouse attempted to lower his head, only to be poked again by the Rabbit.

"I say, listen to me," the Rabbit urged. "You are good with riddles, and I have one for you."

The little rodent raised his head and smiled drowsily. "I *am* good at riddles," he mumbled. "I read a lot, and I sleep a lot, too. Makes me good at thinking."

"Yes, yes," interrupted the Rabbit impatiently. "My riddle is this: What is it when servants are both loyal and traitors to the Crown?"

"Oh, that is a riddle," said the mouse, one eye widening at the prospect of it. "Let us see. Well, first the servants would have to love the Crown and not hate it. You could not have both if that were not true, could you?"

"No, I suppose not. And I *do*... I mean, the *servants* do love the Crown, after all. That is what makes the riddle so hard."

"Yes, yes, I can see that." The mouse's other eye squinted as the first eye opened wider. "So if the servants love the Crown, but they still are traitors to the Crown, why I think they must want someone new to be on the throne. Would that be right?"

"Someone new? I had not thought about someone *new*... There are already three, is that not enough?"

"Oh, I mean do away with the others for someone new," said the Dormouse. "I believe the answer to your riddle must be a revolt. To be both loyal to the Crown and be traitors as well could only mean the servants are in revolt."

The mouse's head jerked up. "Oh dear! Do you think there is a revolt coming against the King?"

"Oh no, oh no," stammered the Rabbit quickly. "Not against the *King*. No, most definitely not."

Thinking quickly, the Rabbit stood up and made an exaggerated effort to look over the hedge. "Oh, I believe they are looking for you again," he told the mouse. "Must get back to the game now."

The Dormouse sighed and stretched. "Suppose I must. I would not want the King to start looking for someone else to do my job. I might find myself being court martialed again." The small rodent made a visible effort to jump a few times in place, then raced off back through the hedge. "Good luck, Rabbit!" he called as he ran.

But the Rabbit was no longer listening. "A revolt." He rolled the word across his tongue, testing the sound of it. "Perhaps not a revolt, but instead a revolution." The Rabbit reached up and pulled at his whiskers thoughtfully. "Yes, yes, I see that now. If I am both an enemy but servant to the Crown, I could only be a revolutionary. Because I could not be a traitor if I serve the Crown. I just need to *change* who wears the Crown, and then I would be a hero instead. That would solve *everything!*"

Without thinking about it, the Rabbit's left hand reached down and pulled his pocket watch free of its pocket and opened it to see the time. Then he stopped and stared first at the watch, and then at the area of his breast plate that had always – and still – covered his pocket and watch.

The watch was indeed in his hand, and the plate was still where it had always been. And yet, now the watch *was* in his hand and *not* in the pocket under the metal plate. It was almost as if the plate metal had ceased to exist for a moment and his hand had passed right through.

Thoughts of revolution momentarily forgotten, the Rabbit continued to stare at the face of his pocket watch, a part of him hoping that this was not yet another problem he was going to be forced to solve.

Chapter 2

Digging Holes

Betsy Bobbin had only been an innocent thirteen-year-old Oklahoma girl when she had first found herself in the Land of Oz. Since then however, she had come to consider herself quite worldly – at least as far as the realm of Oz was concerned. She had seen nomes, witches, several enchanted beings brought to life with magic and all manner of talking beasts. In fact, even her best friend, Hank the Mule, had learned to speak after coming to Oz. But none of those experiences had ever involved *digging* to find an adventure.

Yet that was precisely what the men below were doing. Led by what appeared to be Oz's own standing army – for the twenty some-odd individuals in mismatched uniforms leading the work below could only be Ozma's very own generals, colonels, majors and captains – many of the local workmen had been conscripted into digging into the barren soil of the land. It was not entirely clear why they would be digging in this isolated area of Gilliken Country, but nevertheless, there they were. Dorothy's favorite metal bodyguard, Tik-Tok, could be seen occasionally moving about from one area of the work site to another, using his considerable strength wherever it could be used. Betsy even saw Omby Amby, Ozma's own personal bodyguard and Captain-General of the entire army, walking about at one point, his tall stature and his great green moustache visible over the heads of all he walked past.

Of course, as was quite common with Ozma's army, none of the officers seemed to be engaged in the work itself. None of the officers resembled each other, and – though each wore an elaborate uniform – none matched another. Yet they all somehow knew each others' rank and where they fell within the order of command, even if it was not immediately obvious to anyone else. And so they had no difficulty in passing commands amongst themselves and down the line to the workers actually doing the labor. If either of the two privates left under the officers were present, Betsy had not yet spotted them.

For years, the young girl had been the constant companion of Dorothy Gale of Kansas, traveling on one adventure after another. She quickly became fast friends with Dorothy after arriving in the Emerald City, but even to a naive thirteen year old, it was clear that she was little more than a substitute for the true girl of Dorothy's heart, Princess Ozma. Dorothy and Ozma had an intimate relationship long before Betsy arrived, yet Ozma's duties as the ruler of Oz coupled with the Kansas girl's wanderlust kept the two apart for weeks at a time. Betsy's arrival seemed to fill a necessary role in both girls' lives – for Dorothy, the constant companion to travel about with, and to Ozma, in knowing that Dorothy would never be alone.

Betsy's place in Oz was set even further when Ozma named her a princess of Oz. It made her effectively second in line to inherit the Emerald Throne behind Dorothy, but since no one ever really died in Oz, it was more an honorary title than anything else.

The girl had never experienced the kinds of affection Dorothy showered her with before, either. Though Betsy was actually a year older than the Kansas girl, she lacked Dorothy's experiences. Betsy was still quite shy when she came to Oz, while Dorothy was the polar opposite, very outgoing. To find herself the subject of such intense fondness simply overwhelmed Betsy's senses. The consequence was that she fell quite quickly – and quite madly – in love with Dorothy almost from the beginning.

It was the intensity of these emotions that blinded Betsy to the truth for so many years. While she knew of Dorothy's divided affections, sharing herself with both Ozma and the new girl in her life, there was always an uncomfortable aspect in how Dorothy did share. When she was in the Emerald City, the Kansas girl's attention was focused upon Ozma – as much as the Crown Princess could spare her own time for Dorothy. When Dorothy was away on one adventure or another, she spent an equal amount of energy fawning over Betsy.

But over time, it became abundantly clear that Dorothy's true love was Ozma. Though Dorothy was certainly never cruel about it, nevertheless, her affections for Betsy were only acted upon when Ozma herself was not available. If the crowned princess of Oz were, Betsy would find herself alone or, at the very least, outside the conversation entirely.

Except for Hank, of course. Betsy could always rely upon her mule friend for company. Hank, though, was not Dorothy, and that would make even Hank uncomfortable after awhile. In a sense, Hank was relegated in her own life to where Betsy herself was in Dorothy's – important enough for company only when the object of her affection was unavailable.

Dorothy could not help where her heart lay. Betsy knew this. But it did not make the sting of rejection any less painful once Betsy allowed herself to see it for what it was. And it was many years further on before Betsy decided to do anything about it. Whether Betsy were Dorothy's first choice or not, she at least was *one* of Dorothy's choice, which meant that whenever Ozma was not about, Betsy could bask in Dorothy's love for herself. And Betsy did so love Dorothy.

Both girls were well grown by the time Betsy finally decided to step away from the relationship. In Oz, there were no seasons nor any real way to tell the passage of time unless one counted the days altogether. And somehow, that seemed a pointless endeavor when no one really aged all that much in the faery land in the first place. However, both Dorothy and Betsy visibly appeared to be young women – perhaps seventeen or eighteen – when Betsy made a choice to walk away.

Betsy could remember it plainly enough, even on this day so far removed from the Emerald City. Ozma had decided to go on one of her rare tours of Oz and visit a retreat in the hills of Quadling Country to the south. It was announced as an official duty of the crown, but in truth it was an effort for Dorothy and the Crown Princess to have some privacy. Betsy was present when the two had made the announcement in the Emerald City's great square. Dorothy had not even mentioned the excursion to her, but the Kansas girl was not at all been surprised by Ozma's announcement, so she plainly knew about it. Once again, Betsy was left on the outside looking in, which by itself would have been so much like prior times that Betsy would likely have simply accepted it as such.

But Dorothy – perhaps responding to some internal compass that sensed Betsy's discomfort – took notice of the Oklahoma girl beside her. Forcefully calming the excitement she plainly felt, Dorothy asked in a somewhat distracted manner whether Betsy would like to come along with her and Ozma. Betsy could tell from the way Dorothy asked that she was only being polite, and that the Kansas girl had not really thought that far ahead. As was Dorothy's manner, the girl was only being nice to her companion: offering, yet at the same time hoping – perhaps even expecting – Betsy to decline.

And Betsy did decline. She shook her head sweetly, her mop of yellow curls bouncing in such a way as to hide the tears she barely kept hidden. Dorothy returned the smile by reflex, but was then once again focused on Ozma.

Betsy could have left then and Dorothy was likely not to notice. She did not though. She waited patiently while Ozma and Dorothy mounted the Crown Princess' carriage drawn by the Sawhorse, Ozma's most inelegantly shaped yet pleasant wooden horse. Betsy stood and waved with all the other citizens as the two rode through the gates of the city and out onto the Yellow Brick Road. Yes, the girl from Oklahoma played her part one last time.

But as soon as the gates were closed behind them, Betsy dropped her arm and all pretense. She made her way to her rooms in the Emerald Palace, packed herself a travel bag and went to the stables to retrieve Hank. She did not wait another day. She of course was now too large to actually ride Hank for any long distance, as Hank was small for his size and Betsy had grown since their earlier adventures. Yet the girl and her mule walked out of the Emerald City that day side by side and began their own adventures – ones which would not always include Dorothy.

Betsy did not banish herself forever from the Emerald City, of course. Nor did she never see Dorothy ever again. But that was the last day that Hank and her had lived there, and it was the end of the carefree days of her youth spent alongside Dorothy as her constant companion.

These days, Betsy lived in Gillikin Country in the north of Oz with Hank, and occasionally in the company of her good friends, Shaggy Man and his brother. Shaggy Man's brother had established a mine in the hills somewhere about, and both he and Shaggy Man mined it on occasion. But whenever the two wished for company, it would quite often be to Betsy's own little cabin that they would come. Her home was remote, but not so much so that it was difficult to find.

Yesterday though her solitude had been interrupted by the arrival of Oz's army. They had been stationed in Gillikin Country for awhile now, several years actually. Ozma apparently sent them north to keep her citizens safe from wild beasts. In that time, they occasionally passed by and on even rarer occasion stopped and engaged in conversation. So their appearance in and of itself was not a great surprise.

The army had marched past her home without a comment and set off over a nearby hill. From her home, Besty could hear them arguing amongst themselves but nothing more. At first, this was all they seemed to be interested in doing. Betsy was well enough aware of this behavior and left them to their own devices. She had learned long ago that attempting to get in the way of Oz's officers would be more likely to cause her trouble than to resolve anything. For all their bright colors, the truth was that the officers were largely cowardly and they were always looking for others to do the actual military work.

But upon waking today, Hank informed her that the army had gone about recruiting local farmers and workers to begin digging a hole.

"Whatever for?" had asked Betsy.

Hank had shrugged. "Not that I would know," responded her friend. "Makes as much sense as anything else they do."

Betsy could not disagree, but nevertheless had climbed the nearby hill to look down upon what the army was about. From her vantage point, she could see the broad valley below, but the dust kicked up by the work made it difficult to see either how large the hole was they were working on, or even what purpose the hole could possibly serve.

"I believe that could be something," said Hank, extending his right front leg forward to indicate a direction. By this point, most of the day had already passed, and though the work site was beginning to take shape from the higher vantage point, the reason for digging what was quickly becoming a massive pit in the ground was still not plain.

Betsy squinted in the direction Hank indicated and soon saw the object of the mule's attention. At first, wisps of dust blew past, blocking the view, but as wind gusted through the valley, Betsy could finally see the dark stones that Hank had seen come into view. Deep in one of the holes being dug, the army's workforce had apparently discovered some kind of building.

"I never knew anyone in Oz being interested in digging up old buildings before," commented Betsy. "Before I came to Oz, I remember people talking about doing things like that. Digging up cities and graves and things, but never here."

Hank cocked his head inquisitively. "Why would people do that?"

"To learn things, I think," answered Betsy. "People would write books about what they would find. I never read them, but I heard about them."

Hank kicked his hoof in the dirt. "Seems a waste of time to me," he said. "Leave what's buried alone, I say."

"In this instance, you would be right," came a voice from behind the pair.

Betsy jumped and turned around to see an old woman leading a group of people up the hill towards them from below. The girl's eye immediately caught upon the tall metal man walking close behind the old woman, and called out in recognition. "Nick Chopper!" Then her eyes turned upon the rest, and spotted others she knew. "Glinda! And Sawhorse! What a surprise!"

Hank snorted lightly beside her, but Betsy was certain it was not loud enough for anyone to hear. There had been a small rivalry between Hank and the Sawhorse since the two first came to Oz all those years ago. It had started as a simple bragging contest between Hank, the Sawhorse, the Cowardly Lion and the Hungry Tiger over which of the three girls were the best mistress – Ozma, Dorothy or Betsy.

That disagreement was settled rather quickly on that day, but over time there remained something of a grudge between the Sawhorse and Hank. It was never spoken of, as far as Betsy knew, but she could not help but catch the occasional sign from Hank that he was not happy being around the Sawhorse. The magical wooden creature did not seem to share Hank's negative feelings, but to be honest, it would have been extremely difficult to read the wooden construct's body language to know.

Along with those Betsy knew, two others came up the hill, as well – the old woman who had apparently first addressed them and another young woman with blond hair and a lovely blue dress with white stockings.

"It is good to see you, Betsy Dear," called Glinda as she approached. "It has been far too long since you and Hank have graced the Emerald City."

Betsy did her best to look unaffected by the Good Witch's words, but there was no mistaking the underlying message. *Dorothy* missed having Betsy in the Emerald City, and Glinda likely knew through use of her Great Book of Records precisely what had come between the two princesses of Oz. It was an uncomfortable reminder that though Glinda was a Good Witch, there was no such thing as privacy where she was concerned.

Once the small band reached the top of the hill, Betsy moved forward to hug Glinda, setting aside her discomfort at the witch's words. "It *is* good to see you."

Taking a step back, Glinda provided introductions. "You of course know Nick Chopper and the Sawhorse, but may I provide introduction to our new friend, Alice Liddell of Ox-ford," at this, Glinda nodded toward the girl in blue, who did a quick curtsy as way of greeting, "and to our – companion – Alasia."

It did not escape Betsy's keen mind that Glinda provided only the older woman's name, but she chose not to press the point just yet. Instead, Betsy decided to ask the more obvious questions first.

"What brings you to Gillikin Country, Glinda? Are you here with the army?"

Glinda's face turned somber. "Straight to it then," she said. "Though I have not seen it with my own eyes, I can tell you likely what it is they are trying to uncover. They are trying to find the castle of the former Wicked Witch of the North."

There had been four Wicked Witches at one time, Betsy knew, but they had all been overthrown long before she herself came to Oz. In fact, even Dorothy had only encountered two of them – the ones of the East and West. This was the first mention she could recall of the Wicked Witch of the North. Somehow, the stories involving the witches of the South and North had never been told to her.

"Why would the army be trying to find the castle of a Wicked Witch?" asked Betsy.

"Because they are Ozma's army, and they do as Ozma commands," provided the old woman, Alasia. "Only in this case, the have no idea what they are really doing."

Betsy addressed the older woman herself. "You said something about Hank being right about leaving this building buried? Why? If it's just a castle, that does not seem too much to worry about. I am sure there's nothing inside that can hurt anyone if it's been buried a long time."

Alasia raised an eyebrow while squinting her other eye, a clear sign of irritation. "What do they teach you children when you are young?"

"Alasia," scolded Glinda. "Be kind."

"I am," insisted the old woman, taking a step back. "Is it my fault this girl does not understand anything about magic?"

"Alasia," repeated Glinda, holding the old woman's stare.

At this point, the girl whom Glinda had introduced as Alice stepped forward. "Do forgive Alasia, as she is not used to working with others, I am told." The girl extended her hand. "I am Alice," she provided, even though Glinda had introduced her but moments before.

Betsy took the hint, taking the girl's hand in her own. "I am Betsy. And this is my friend, Hank the Mule."

Alice curtsied again, this time facing Hank. "Why hello, Hank. Are you able to speak as do so many of the animals in this place?"

"Of course," scoffed the mule, though Betsy could detect the slightest hint of pride in her friend's voice. Too many people took the mule for granted, and this girl's simple manner complimented him in a way few ever had before.

Rising, Alice looked past Betsy to the work below. "Glinda is right, of course. That does look like the other castle I saw earlier."

Betsy followed Alice's line of sight, where she could also begin to make out the shape of a castle's spire. The dark stone made it appear somewhat shapeless amidst the dust, but once she had an idea of what to look for, the shape was unmistakable.

"But why are you all here to watch them unbury an old castle?"

"Oh, we are not here to watch them," said Alasia. "We are here to stop them. They cannot be allowed to unbury Mombi's old castle. I can't say for certain what it is she wants inside those walls, but whatever it is, it would be a very bad idea to let her have it."

"Who?" asked Betsy confused. "Mombi? The old lady from the Emerald City? The Wizard's friend? She would hardly be someone I would worry about."

Alasia cackled, earning her another glare from Glinda.

"You likely were not told, but Mombi used to be the Wicked Witch of the North, Betsy," explained the Good Witch. "I took her power away and Ozma was kind enough to let her live out her days in the Emerald City. But somehow, Mombi has gained her powers back and she wants to get control of her old castle again. So she has tricked the army into unearthing it."

"I thought you said the army was doing this because Ozma told them to?" Betsy's brow furled as she tried to make sense of what the Good Witch was explaining.

"This is where things become difficult," said Nick for the first time.

"Yes," agreed Glinda. "You see, Mombi's power was to change her shape. She could become anyone or anything, and could change other people and things, as well. It seems that while we were away from the Emerald City looking for her, Mombi has taken Ozma's place. It is not Ozma who apparently sits upon the Emerald Throne – it is the Wicked Witch of the North in disguise."

Betsy gasped, covering her mouth. She cast a worried look to Hank, but she could not glean the mule's impression of the news. Despite their history, Betsy had never wished ill upon the Crown Princess. In fact, she still considered Ozma a friend, even if she were her emotional rival for Dorothy's affections.

"What has happened to Ozma?" managed the girl from Oklahoma at last.

Glinda gave a heavy sigh. "We do not know," she answered sadly. "We just do not know."

Chapter 3

Witch Under Glass

"There *must* be a way. There must!"

Dorothy continued to pace back and forth in the vast chamber that encompassed the entire top floor of the castle. What was clearly a replica or a version of the Wyrd Castle in Wonderland, this castle was equally as vacant as any of the others that looked like it that could be found in Oz. No creature seemed to walk its halls – not even an insect. And certainly no witches nor wizards, either.

There was a riddle here, of that Dorothy was certain. Some explanation, some underlying *reason* why there were now four castles in three different faery realms that all looked precisely the same. Yet whatever reason there was, it certainly escaped her mind no matter how she wrestled with the puzzle.

The girl came to a halt once again in the middle of the chamber. For more times than she could recall, Dorothy had counted on her fingers as she attempted to reason out the castle mystery.

"There are two castles in Oz," she said out loud, tapping at the index and middle finger of her right hand. "But the Wizard says those are copies of the Wyrds' castle in Wonderland." At this, she tapped the tip of her ring finger. "And now there is this one behind the mirror in Alice's study." She pinched the tip of her pinkie finger, holding it firmly as she thought more on the subject.

"Everything makes sense *except* this castle." Dorothy scrunched her brow. "Could the one in Wonderland *also* be a copy? Or could this one be *another* copy?"

Dropping her hands to her side, she let out a great sigh. "And how does any of this help me contact the Wizard?"

Of course, that had not been the original plan upon coming here. The Wizard had surmised that the spell which had fractured Wonderland must exist here. It was a story Alice had read when she had come here, one about a senseless, impossible battle with a Jabberwock – whatever that was supposed to be. The Wizard had guessed that the story itself was, in fact, the spell – and to reverse it and save Wonderland, the spell would need to be brought back to him. Upon retrieving the book, Dorothy was supposed to return to Wonderland through the Rabbit's Hole.

All of that had changed once Dorothy had discovered there was another castle here in the place beyond the looking glass, as Alice called it. The Wizard's plan rested upon the belief that the Wyrds – or the Wicked Witches, as they were known in Oz – had cast the spell from the castle in Wonderland, and this was from where any spell to undo their damage must also be cast. And yet – if the castle itself had also been copied, was the Wizard truly in the proper place to cast the spell?

The girl from Kansas had managed to travel to this castle, believing it to be a magical reflection of the castle in Wonderland. If that were true, she should have been able to find a mirror and use that to see into Wonderland and to contact the Wizard. That hope had been banished however when she had actually found a small, hand-held mirror, though – when she attempted to use the mirror to look through it and into Wonderland, she had instead somehow activated something else entirely. Instead of the Wizard, she had found herself in direct contact with one of the Wicked Witches of Oz!

This alone would have been frightening enough – except that all of the Wicked Witches, with the exception of Mombi, were supposed to be dead. One had died before the girl had ever come to Oz, another had been banished, one she had dropped her house upon and the final one she had melted with a pail of water. So where was this *new* Wicked Witch from? Alice had mentioned that Mombi had somehow gotten loose with new magic and that someone else was posing as a Wicked Witch, as well. Was this the new one that Alice had mentioned, or someone else entirely?

Which had bred an even scarier thought – if the castles could be reflected between faery realms, could the witches have, as well? Could there be four *duplicate* witches, and if so, where were they?

Dorothy had dropped the mirror she had accidentally contacted the Wicked Witch through, shattering it upon the ground. So any chance of using the mirror to try to discover any of those answers was gone. But also was any chance she had of trying to reach the Wizard.

Armed with this fear, the girl had set out to search the rest of the castle in hopes of finding another mirror she could use. And there were several to be found, though all were mounted upon walls and impossible to move about. Also, none of them could be used to see anything other than her own reflection.

It was when Dorothy's search finally brought her to the very top of the castle that she had begun to feel frustrated. She had searched both high and low in the castle and learned nothing. She still had the book she had come for, and she could certainly return to the mirror to exit the Looking Glass World – but some part of her knew that if she left, whatever this castle represented might well be lost, as well.

Though Alice had not mentioned it specifically, she did suggest that she had only made one trip through the mirror in the study. Considering how much Alice had longed to go on another adventure, if the girl had been able to return through the mirror, surely she would have. And if she did not, that could only mean that she *could* not.

With that reasoning, Dorothy had no choice but to believe that once she left this Looking Glass World, she would never again be able to return. And anything the castle could have done to help their cause would be lost. Especially if this was truly where the spell was cast from, and where any spell to undo it needed to be used.

"I sure wish Toto were here," said Dorothy. "Or any of my friends. Especially the Scarecrow – he could've reasoned this all out by now for sure."

Without any other place to go, Dorothy once again descended the stairs. The only thing of any interest she had discovered in all this massive castle had been the mirror through which she had seen the Wicked Witch. It was the only place she had seen any sign that contact with the world beyond the looking glass was even possible. This was the only place Dorothy could think to go.

In truth, once the girl had left the study where she had found the mirror, she had shied away from going back. The idea of running into the Wicked Witch herself, or of accidentally letting the witch see her again, frightened her. She had never had to face one the witches completely on her own before. Though she had been the one to cast the water upon the Wicked Witch of the West, it had not been something she had planned – she had only thrown the bucket of water at the witch because she had tricked Dorothy into removing one of her silver slippers. She had not set out to fight the old woman; the fact that the witch was allergic to water had been completely unknown to the little girl.

In all her years of adventures, Dorothy had never had to face anyone as powerful as the witches were said to have been. Even the Nome King and all his armies were not as fearsome as the Wicked Witches, who had held all of Oz in fear for so many years before Dorothy had come along. And each time she had defeated one – first by being in the house that dropped upon the Wicked Witch of the East, and then in melting the Wicked Witch of the West – it had been completely unintentional. So to plan on facing one head on without any real knowledge of how to defeat them without a new house to drop or bucket of water to throw was truly unnerving to the otherwise brave girl.

But so far, the only other person she had managed to contact was from within that study, and so it was there she would need to return.

When Dorothy reached the door to the room, she paused only briefly, taking a deep breath before forcing herself to pull the door open and enter.

The room had not changed any since she had left, but that was no real surprise. She was, after all, the only one who could have changed anything here. Even the witch she had been so fearful of was somewhere else.

The chamber was still cluttered with papers, books and various knick-knacks cast about with very little organization. There were shelves along the walls where some degree of order had once existed, but it was apparent that whatever system used to organize the books had long since been abandoned. It was under scattered sheets of paper that Dorothy had originally found the mirror, and who knew what else lay hidden under the remaining objects scattered about the room.

Beside the table on the floor, the girl could plainly see the shattered remains of the mirror she had dropped. And though small device seemed completely normal, she made a careful effort to avoid where it lay upon the ground as she set about her search of the chamber.

Rifling through this room however proved equally as fruitless as searching the rest of the castle. Another mirror was revealed beneath a tapestry along one wall, and though it was a large, free-standing mirror, it was still too cumbersome to move. At best, Dorothy could manage to tilt the mirror slightly, but nothing was displayed in the reflection other than the room and herself.

Exhausted, Dorothy fell heavily into the pillowed chair placed beside the window. Out the window, she could see out over the landscape, covered beneath a blanket of white snow. At the edge of the view, she could make out the house that had served as her entryway into this backwards world, but the building hid whatever else lay beyond it. Part of her had hoped to spot the Red King or Queen wandering about, but if they were, they were too far away to be seen.

Dorothy felt her eyes getting heavy. Her mind became clouded as she found herself wondering how long it had been since she had slept. Certainly before she had left Oz. But there had been no darkness to signal evening, and so she had been running constantly on this adventure. *Do Wonderland or this Looking Glass World even have nighttime?* she wondered.

Girl.

Dorothy's eyes snapped open. There had been a voice... Had it been a dream?

Girl, come here.

No missing it this time – there had been a voice. A strangely resonating vibration that had formed words. A woman's voice.

I know you are there, girl. I can see you there at the edge of the glass.

Dorothy looked around the room, a pit of fear in her heart as she realized who must be speaking. Her fear was made manifest when she caught sight of an old woman standing to the back of the room, surrounded by a sickly green mist.

But no – she was not standing, as Dorothy had first thought. She was not even fully there. The woman's reflection was suspended within the frame of the large mirror the girl had uncovered in her search. The mirror was not even fully facing where Dorothy sat, though that was only because the girl had moved the mirror in her search. Had she not, the girl believed the mirror would have been facing her seat directly.

The woman in the mirror gave an exaggerated grunt. *I mean you no harm, girl. Come, let me have a look at ye.*

Dorothy remained rooted in her chair for a moment, looking about the room in search of any other threat which might have appeared. When none were immediately visible, Dorothy leaned forward in her chair.

"Which one are you?" the girl asked, screwing up her confidence. "You're one of the Wicked Witches, I can guess that much. But which one?"

The old woman in the mirror cackled. *I will tell you all you wish, but first you must come where I can see you properly.*

The girl from Kansas considered for a moment, then stood and walked to where she faced the mirror at a more direct angle, though she deliberately remained on the opposite side of the room.

"Better?"

Oh, much. The old woman made a show of looking the girl up and down. *Yes, yes. You are the girl. Yes indeed. Older, but you are the one who melted me.*

Dorothy felt herself jump slightly at the words. She had only melted one witch – but this was not her.

"That was the Wicked Witch of the West," the girl rebutted. "I've never lain eyes upon you before."

So formal, scoffed the old woman. *But you may call me by my true name. We are old friends, you and I.*

"I don't know your name," insisted Dorothy. "As I have said, I don't know you."

Oh, I only look different, Dearie. I am still the witch who you melted with water when you took my home from me.

Dorothy was at a loss as for what to say. Finally, she burst out, "I didn't know the water would melt her. I swear. But it did, and it stopped her from being mean to the Winkies, so it wasn't all a bad thing."

I am not here to speak of right or wrong, girl, scolded the old woman. *Whether you believe me or not, I am here to help you.*

"Help me?" Dorothy could not hide the laugh in her voice. "If you are who you say, you beat my friends terribly and locked up myself, Toto and the Cowardly Lion in your castle. Why would I ever believe you are here to help me now?"

Only because you have something I need, and if you would agree to help me with it, I will in turn help you.

"I hardly think that there is anything I would want to help you with," said Dorothy guardedly.

Hmmm. The witch ran her hand over her chin. *Perhaps if you told me how I can help you, and I do what you need done, I can prove my good will?*

"How do you know I even need anything?" asked Dorothy. In truth, Dorothy really could not imagine anything a Wicked Witch could help her with anyways.

I know you wished to speak to someone else when you first reached out to me, cooed the Wicked Witch. *I imagine you have not been able to speak with him yet, as you are still there and only I can use the magic of my mirrors. So if I were to help you speak with whomever it is you wished to, would that not show I speak true?*

Dorothy pondered that thought a moment before responding. "That *would* be helpful," admitted Dorothy. Yet at the same time, she thought, *Only you'd hear whatever the Wizard and I said, so that would* not *be helpful.*

Almost as if the witch could read Dorothy's thoughts, she said, *I could teach you to use one of my mirrors to call your friend. And then you would know that I cannot listen in.*

The Kansas girl cast that idea about in her mind, but could find no flaw in it. If she were the one using the mirror, the witch would not be privy to the conversation between herself and the Wizard. It seemed like a legitimate offer.

"Okay," said the girl. "If I were to agree to that, what would you want from me?"

The old woman's face sunk visibly. *You are in my home, Dearie. My castle. I have not been able to be there in many, many years. Almost anything you could bring me from there would have more value than anything I have here.*

"But you want something specific, don't you?"

The old woman nodded. *Yes, I do. But not for a reason you might think. I need the looking glass that you first spoke to me with. It is my most special belonging, for it is the glass I brought with me when first I entered the Land as a little girl. I only want it for the memories, for nothing more. It is special to me.*

"I-- I broke it," admitted Dorothy. "By accident, but I dropped it. You startled me and, well..." The girl shrugged, looking down toward the shattered pieces lying on the ground between herself and the larger mirror.

I knew that much already, said the witch. *I know when a glass can no longer be used, and since I cannot imagine how you could have taken the magic from it, having it broken was the reasonable conclusion. But that does not matter. All I need is the frame. The glass can be reforged. Just leave the glass where it lies. All you need do is take the frame with you when you leave my castle and bring it to me in Oz.*

Dorothy found her spirits lift slightly before she reminded herself what it is she was planning to do. Everything the witch suggested seemed perfectly reasonable. But it was *still* making a deal with one of the Wicked Witches. And she could not imagine anything good that could come of such a bargain.

Suddenly, an idea seized the girl's mind. "Before I agree, you need to answer something for me."

The old woman's face scowled a moment before relaxing into an obviously strained effort of solicitude. *Name your query, girl.*

"I have been hearing all kinds of stories about you and your other witches. About how you really came from Wonderland, and about how you built all your castles in Oz like you did in Wonderland, right?"

I do not know this 'Wonderland', girl. But it is true that my sisters and I come from the Land, which is another faery realm where we had castles like what we have in Oz, yes. Was that your question?

"No," said Dorothy quickly, filing away the idea that the witches had castles in Wonderland – plural, not just one. "I have also heard that you escaped Wonderland-- er, the Land, by casting a spell. You made a story real that could not *be* real."

The old woman nodded, her eyes squinting as she absorbed how much Dorothy knew. *Yes...* The old woman's voice dripped with menace.

"Okay, so if all that is true, did you cast the spell from here in your castle or somewhere else?"

Why would you ever need to know such a thing? asked the Wicked Witch, her suspicion plain upon her face.

"To be honest, I don't really," responded Dorothy. And in truth, *she* did not. But the Wizard did. The girl did not like to tell lies, but she reasoned this was not truly a lie in the end, because it was true that she was not the one in need of the information. "But I think it would be a good way to tell if you're really telling me the truth. If you don't want to tell me, then I'll know you are up to something."

The old woman in the mirror began to fade away a moment behind her green mist, but after a moment her image clarified again. *Very well. None of us could agree on whose castle to use. So we used none. We found a place that was an equal distance from all our castles and we made the story real there.*

"Does this place have a name?"

No. It was just a place in the open. No place that mattered. All that did was assure that none of us was seen as being in charge, or as being closer to our centers of power than another. Even if it was Mombi's idea, none of us would have gone along if any one of us would have gained more than another from it.

Dorothy nodded as though she completely understood all that had been said, even if a good portion of it she did not. But the Wizard had said that time was running short...

"Very well," said Dorothy finally. "If you'll help me speak with the Wizard, then I'll bring you your mirror frame. Is that the deal?"

The old witch nodded, a smile creeping into the corner of her mouth. *Yes, yes. That is all I ask.*

Dorothy could tell from the witch's reaction that there was more to this, but whatever the witch had planned, it was beyond her understanding. And besides – she would be seeing the Wizard before returning to Oz, and he would be a better judge of whether to give up the prize before they ever returned there. So there was plenty of time to reconsider the deal.

At last, Dorothy nodded her head in compliance. "So show me how to talk to the Wizard."

Chapter 4

Mirrored Plans

The man known by far too many as the Wizard Oz, even though his real name was Oscar Diggs, felt frazzled. Time was running out for finding an answer, and he was no closer now than when he had first begun his search. Even a visit from the Cheshire Cat – who typically could be counted on for at the very *least* a fragment of usable information if one had but the patience to weed through his otherwise pointless ramblings – had helped him not at all.

This was not to say that the cat had not provided information. As always, there were pearls scattered about all he said. What frustrated the Wizard most of all was that the information did not help him in the least with his current dilemma. And none of his other plans were working out, either.

Oscar had sent Dorothy to the faery land that apparently existed behind a mirror in Christ Church in Oxford England, a land that all evidence suggested was actually a shard of the world he presently occupied, the world that Alice had called Wonderland. He had sent her there after a book that Alice reported contained the story of the Jabberwock, an impossible creature made real somehow by the Wyrds as a way to escape their captivity here in Wonderland. Only, a good amount of time had passed, and he had heard nothing from Dorothy – and that worried him, as well.

The task he had sent her on should have been an easy one: go into the room on the other side of the mirror, find the book, and return through the mirror. Then all she would need to do was travel to the Rabbit's Hole, which by all reports was at the edge of the gardens, and return to Wonderland. Once here, simply choosing the Wyrds' Castle as a location should have brought her back in a short time. In all, Oscar had planned upon perhaps a couple hours worth of effort – only by now, three times that much had passed, and still there was no word from Dorothy.

In the meantime, the old man had searched through every conceivable book within the castle's disorderly library, searching for anything that might be of help. He had certainly learned a great deal – what color was the best to think of when you were trying to sew; the worst recipe for rock and stone pie; even a diagram for predicting the weather inside a nutshell – but nothing that in any way related to the spell that the Wyrds had cast. After all, simply possessing the story itself was only part of the solution – he needed to know what magic was used to make the story real. And if he could not locate that piece of information, Dorothy's mission beyond the mirror would be completely misspent.

Some time ago, the Wizard had collapsed into the only relaxing chair in the room – a red cushioned piece positioned by the only window in the room. The other two were wooden jobs that could barely pass the definition of a chair, and were only good for sitting at the tables for reading – and for ruining an old man's back. The view from the window showed the room's level was at just the right height to see over the peaks of the trees which surrounded the castle so that he actually had a commanding view over the entire valley. But it did nothing to give him any comfort about his problem.

Dorothy's new-found companion, the log she had named Bark, had long ago run off, presumably to explore the rest of the castle. But what did one know of the motive of chunks of chopped lumber that acted like pet dogs? The best one could do to predict such a creature was to guess its motives based upon what a real dog might do in the same situation. Oscar had never been one to have pets – save for the collection of mini-piglets he had kept in his pocket to perform one of his slight of hand illusions – but if there was one thing he knew about dogs, it was that they would run off if you ever left a gate open for them. And the old man had deliberately left the door to the castle's library wide open once the imitation canine had bounded one too many times onto the table in front of him.

Oscar had come to Wonderland to find a weakness for the Wicked Witches of Oz, who had come originally from this place when they were known simply as Wyrds. The arrival of Dorothy and, shortly after, the girl Alice, had changed his focus somewhat. By learning that his own spell that had brought him to Wonderland had also brought him back in time, he reasoned that this Wonderland place must not exist anymore in his own time, which meant there was no way to know how long he had until this realm simply ceased to exist altogether. The only thing he could be certain of is that it *would* come to an end, and the presumption was that it would be soon. For why else would his magic have brought him back to this time precisely?

The Cheshire's visit had confirmed some of that, at least. This place had been shattered by the Wyrds' magic, because when they left, they had taken the land's fate with them – whatever that meant. The cat had not said those words directly, but the truth was, if one did not seek to unravel the Cheshire's words, one would never understand a single word the creature said in the first place.

But the more frightening aspect which the cat had revealed was that there had been more than one castle in Wonderland. And if the feline was to be believed, only this one remained. Which meant that this may very well *not* have been where Oscar needed to search at all – what he needed could very likely have been in one of the other three castles, and all the time he had spent here had been a complete and absolute waste of time.

Unfortunately, the Wizard's continued search had largely proven that notion to be true. Though this library may have been one of the most extensive collections of worthless information he had ever come across, the one piece that this collection did not have was the specific spell that was used to shatter Wonderland.

Apparently, that spell had been lost in one of the shards that had broken away from this place when the Wyrds had escaped.

Which left the Wizard not only in the wrong castle entirely, but trapped in a world he was not entirely certain he could escape from. His magic had brought him here – but the one secret he had not shared with Dorothy was that he had not been able to make all of his magic function within Wonderland. His magic word worked – the one that allowed him to change shape – but not the magic which would allow him to move from place to place. For all intents and purposes, when it came to transportation, the old man was precisely that – a man. A man without any magic immediately at his disposal that he could use to leave this place before it fell to whatever fate awaited it in the near future.

Wizard. Are you there?

Oscar sat up in an instant, looking about for the source of the voice. It had an oddly metallic sound to it – or perhaps not metallic, but certainly it contained an odd vibration that made it sound as though it were not being spoken by a real living person.

Wizard, if you can hear me, please say something. I can't see you at all.

"Dorothy?" asked the Wizard hesitantly. The voice *did* sort of sound like his friend, but it certainly was not the sound of someone who was in the same room with him. His mind flashed back to the sounds he might hear through a telephone, or possibly from a phonograph. But this lacked the grainy quality that those devices produced. This was clear – it just had an odd vibration to it.

Oh, it worked! Wizard, it's me. It's Dorothy!

"Yes, my dear," said the Wizard, standing and looking about the room for where his friend's voice came from. "Where are you at, precisely?"

I am still in the Looking Glass World. I am using one of the Witch's mirrors.

"One of the--" Oscar's eyes rooted on a large draped object across the room and realized immediately what must be behind it. "How-- what-- I don't understand. A witch's, you say?"

As he spoke, the Wizard rushed across the room and pulled the red velvet cover away, revealing a large, full-sized mirror mounted in a swiveled frame. But instead of seeing his own reflection, the Wizard plainly saw the brunette Kansas girl standing where he did in the same room.

A more critical look told the Wizard that it was not exactly the same – there were minor differences visible in the room where Dorothy stood, after all. But the similarities between the two locations were uncanny.

I found another castle, Wizard. Dorothy rushed out. *Another castle here in the Looking Glass World. And it looks just like the one there where you are!*

"I can see that, truly." The Wizard pulled at his chin, trying to reason out the confusion. The cat had said there had originally been four castles – just like what the Wicked Witches had built for themselves in Oz. He had been to Mombi's castle in the north, though in truth he had never been invited to any of the upper story rooms, so he could not say how closely that castle resembled this one. But in truth, in thinking back, there had been some remarkable likenesses to the entryway of this castle.

Could the similarities between *all* the castles been this identical? He could not say without making a more precise examination of all the castles in Oz, but there was certainly a remarkable coincidence in how these two rooms appeared.

It's a long story, continued the mirror-Dorothy. *But--*

The Wizard held up his hand. "Please, Dorothy. You need to calm down and tell me things slowly. Start from the beginning. I can see you found your way to the mirror world Alice spoke of, but did you find the book?"

Dorothy nodded briskly, bending down and holding up a large tome. *Yes, I did. This is it. But Wizard, there's more. This book was written by Mombi!*

Oscar felt sweat bead on his forehead. "By Mombi? Are you sure?"

Her name is on the cover. The girl in the mirror pointed down to a stylized form of writing in the lower corner of the front cover. But Oscar could not make out what the words might be, for they seemed to be written with letters he had never seen before.

"I cannot read that, Dorothy. How is it you can?"

Oh, said the girl, realizing her mistake. *I forgot. You can only see it if you look at it in a mirror. Or if you press it in snow.*

"But I am seeing it in a mirror."

Dorothy scrunched up her face, as she so often did when she was thinking. *I don't think this is the right kind of mirror. You need to see it backwards, and I don't think that is what we are seeing right now.*

Oscar tugged at his chin again. "Very well, I will need to take your word for it then. But this book has the story of the Jabberwock? You're certain?"

Yes. I've read it. Dorothy fumbled at opening the book, presumably to read it to the Wizard, but he held up his hand.

"Not now, Dorothy. Not in this way. We have no way of telling what it might do if spoken aloud. Please, tell me why you did not come back straight away once you had this book?"

I tried. But moving here is not the same. If you walk forward, you end up going backwards. It is as though you skip over where you are and end up where you might have been before. It's all very confusing.

That made sense, mused the Wizard. A mirror world would suggest mirrored action to reaction.

By the time I figured it out, I was outside. And that's where I saw the castle. Another castle, just like in Wonderland. And just like the ones in Oz.

"Yes, it seems there were four of them originally here in Wonderland. I have learned that much." Oscar made a deliberate effort to not mention that he had learned this from the Cheshire Cat. To do that would have required him to both explain the cat's presence – not an easy task to begin with – as well as why anyone should even listen to the creature that no one else even considered sane. "When Wonderland shattered, it seems the other castles broke away, as well.

"I suppose congratulations are in order." The Wizard did his best to paste on a performance worthy smile for the girl's benefit. "You have found one of the lost castles."

Is that important?

"Oh, indeed it is." The old man pondered how to explain his dilemma without losing credibility. "You see, originally we thought there was only one original castle, because that is what everyone here in Wonderland remembers. One castle. And so I assumed this must be where the witches cast their magic from."

Dorothy fairly jumped through the glass at this. *But I know--*

The Wizard held up his hand. "Please, let me finish, Dorothy." He cleared his throat and resumed. "But since I have learned there were four castles, now I am not so certain that the spell was cast here, or even if the spell which was used is even here. We must search all of the castles before we can know for certain from where the spell was cast."

But Wizard--

"Dorothy, *please*," rebuked the Wizard. "Before we can do anything else, we must take advantage of our good fortune that you have found one of these other castles and have you search for what I need. I will give you--"

Wizard! yelled Dorothy.

The girl's uncommon tone startled Oscar. "Oh, what is it?" he blurted without thinking.

The spell was not cast in one of the castles. It was cast outside somewhere. Somewhere equally far from all the castles.

"And how precisely would you know that?"

Because... Dorothy paused at this, chewing at her lower lip. Then she rushed the rest out. *Because the Wicked Witch of the West told me.*

"Fenstel? But is she not dead? You melted her. You said as much."

Is that her name? I never knew it. But yes, she said it was her. Though she didn't look the same, she said I was the one who had melted her. And I've only ever melted one witch. Or anyone else for that matter.

Suddenly, the truth burst free in the Wizard's mind. Reflexively he smacked his palm into his forehead, turning away momentarily from the mirror. "Oh, you stupid, *stupid* old man!"

Wizard, what is it?

Oscar clenched his fists as he faced Dorothy again. "No one can die in Oz! No one! You and I, we come from a world where people die all the time, but after years in Oz, we both should have realized – you could never have killed Fenstel. She could not be killed while she was in Oz. Which means..."

Which means she has been hiding all this time! finished Dorothy.

"Or worse," added the Wizard. "So Fenstel is alive. Which makes two witches to contend with rather than one."

I have never thought to ask before now, but I am beginning to think there is much more about the Wicked Witches you have not told me.

"There is, I admit. But I fear this is not the time to discuss it all. I promise, when we have the time, I will sit down and tell you all I know. But for now, we must be quick about what we do and not dwell upon the witches. That will all come soon enough, I fear."

Oscar stopped himself in mid-thought. "Dorothy." He spoke her name with deliberate slowness. "How is it you came to speak with Fenstel?"

She appeared in the mirror. The one I am using.

"But you are using her mirror. How could you do that if she were not there?"

She showed me how to use the mirror to speak to someone far away. She said that all her mirrors were connected, and that so long as one of hers was near where you were, I could talk to you.

"And why precisely did she tell you that?" The Wizard folded his arms across his chest. "Fenstel has never been known for being at all helpful. She is possibly the most ill-tempered of all the witches, in fact."

I do know that. She trapped me and my friends before, remember?

"So? Why is she willing to help you now? What is she getting out of this?"

Dorothy blanched visibly. *I... I made a deal with her.*

"You did what?!" Oscar was beside himself. "You don't make deals with the witches, Dorothy! I should know. Were you not listening when I told you what happened when I made deals with Mombi?"

I know. But it is only a small thing, and it helped us far more than she even knew. She was the one who told me that the spell was not cast in one of the castles, and that was really important, wasn't it?

The Wizard nodded, but kept his arms folded tightly against his chest. "It is. But what was the cost of this information?"

She wanted her old mirror, is all, explained the girl, leaning out of the frame momentarily and returning with an old hand-held frame. *She knew it was broken, but she said it was important to her. It was something she had when she first came to Wonderland as a little girl.*

"I do not much care for this idea, Dorothy," cautioned Oscar. "Fenstel uses mirrors in her magic. It is part of what lets her see long distances, into places where her telescopic eye alone cannot see. To bring her one that she asks for..."

I understand. I knew it when I agreed. But I needed to speak to you. I needed to know what to do about this place. At this, Dorothy spread her arms around, casting her vision outside the frame of the mirror.

The Wizard unfolded his arms to reach for his chin again. "I don't know, Dorothy. I truly do not. I do need you to search, to look for anything that might resemble the spell the witches used to escape Wonderland. But I honestly cannot say if what we need might not be in your hands there with the book already. I presume the rest of the book is just as unreadable as the cover without a mirror?"

The girl nodded.

"Then we must have you look about your version of the room for any book that might speak of spells involving making something that is *not* real into something that is. And I must see if I can locate a mirror here that I can use to read the book you have there."

Dorothy's head made a quick bob, and she started to walk away from the mirror.

"Oh, one thing more, Dorothy," called the Wizard.

When the girl had returned to the center of the glass, he gave her new instructions.

"I also want you to keep your eyes open for *any* books that talk about cats. In particular, I would like you to find one that talks about how to capture one."

The Kansas girl's face showed surprise. *Does this have anything to do with the Cheshire Cat?*

Oscar's eyebrow shot up. "You know of him?"

Only that I met him before I found you, and that he knew your real name.

"Well, I have reason to believe he knows a great deal more than that," confessed the Wizard. "And I am beginning to believe that before this adventure is done, we will have need of keeping that cat in one place long enough to answer our questions."

Chapter 5

Toto and the Cat

People in Oz were not always predictable. They often ran about doing things that completely confused poor Toto. They would make things important that the small dog could not understand, and completely ignore things that should have been a concern. He was a canine, after all, and he was proud of that fact – and more than once, he had thanked whatever random chance had allowed him to be born that way. For there was far more to being a person than he ever wanted to be involved with.

Give a dog food – even if it needed to be hunted like the Cowardly Lion or Hungry Tiger often claimed to do – and a place to sleep at the end of the day, and everything else would take its place in the world around him. People just added things that made their lives more complicated, and Toto really wanted none of that if he could help it.

No matter how comfortable he was with his own rules in how the world should work, however, Toto found himself too often setting those principles aside for his person, Dorothy. Even if she was just a girl who prided herself on making her life complicated, she was still the closest friend the canine had. And if truth be told, the girl would be lost without him.

Dorothy had a way of making everyone fall in love with her, that much was certain – but there was only one who had been beside her from the beginning, and that was Toto. No matter whether she allowed herself to be called a Princess of Oz, or just a little girl from Kansas, Toto knew that she would always need him to watch out for her. All people tended to ignore the really important things happening all around her – but Dorothy seemed to be involved in so many unnecessary things that there was a significantly greater number of important things that she would overlook every single day. And who else would there be to bring her attention to them if he did not?

Toto had been separated from Dorothy before – there was even a time she came into Oz without him altogether. But he had never been comfortable when he had. No one else watched out for Dorothy – no one else *could* watch out for her – as well as Toto could. No, not even that kitten she had once brought to Oz. He was not at all surprised to learn that the tiny cat had been banished for her part in the disappearance of Ozma's piglet so many years ago – felines were, quite frankly, even more trouble than people were. Of course, if one listened to Eureka herself, it had been she who had asked to go back to Kansas, not Ozma who had cast her out.

But, as with most cats, Eureka did not stay away. She managed to find her way back into Oz – and even managed to change her color in the process. Where once she had been white, she instead had managed to turn herself pink. And, or course, the feline would offer no explanation at all as to how that change came about.

Eureka was taken to wandering off at the most inconvenient times, as well, and placing herself solidly underfoot at even more inopportune moments. Any other time, she simply would lay about being completely worthless. In spite of this, Dorothy and Ozma somehow forgave the cat for her crime that had led to her being banished and acted as though the Pink Kitten had never been cast out of Oz at all. To Toto, it set his scruff on edge to think about.

Thankfully, at some point Eureka decided that someplace else was better to be and stopped coming around the Emerald Palace, which suited Toto just fine. He had seen more than his fair share of cats in Kansas, and he did not much like that one came and went in Oz as she pleased. Toto chose to ignore the idea that the Pink Kitten wandering around Oz on her own was actually even more invasive than her presence around the Emerald Palace, of course – one level of indignity where Eureka was concerned was more than enough.

This left the only feline-like creature he had to deal with being the Glass Cat, who truly was not really a cat at all, anymore than the Sawhorse was really a horse. Bungle the Glass Cat was a magical creation who neither looked nor smelled like any real cat Toto had ever encountered, and though this faux cat was even more obstinate than Eureka in most every way, Toto found the artificial cat's persistent visits to the Emerald City far more palatable than those of the Pink Kitten.

Irregardless, with the Pink Kitten vanished from the palace for many years now, it just represented one less thing the little dog needed to protect Dorothy from.

Except – at present, Toto could not protect Dorothy from anything. Dorothy was missing. Ozma had sent the canine and his person to some faraway garden in search of the Wizard who had gone missing from the Emerald City, and for some inexplicable reason, she only brought Toto back. That left Dorothy wherever she was, and Toto back in the Emerald City without her.

That would have been discouraging enough all on its own. But of course, as misfortune would have it, the territory he had always been vigilant in protecting for Dorothy had been invaded by even more problems than was normal. First he had discovered a cricket and mouse in the palace – which had both just as quickly vanished no matter how far and wide he searched for them. Then Ozma had scolded him for chasing the pests, without giving him the chance to protect even her.

In fact, when he had rushed into Ozma's room, his nose had led him not to the mouse he had been chasing, but to a large emerald hidden in the folds of Ozma's bed – as if the Crown Princess had suddenly taken to sleeping with her gems.

Ever since that night, Ozma had kept her distance from him. At first, the little dog had thought she was upset with him still, and he respected her wishes and stayed some distance away.

This may have been the way it stayed until Dorothy could return and repair whatever rift had formed between Ozma and Toto. But let us not forget – Toto *is* a dog. And dogs, like most animals, have senses people do not. It was these senses which Toto used every single day to watch out for things the people around him never noticed, and it was what gave him the insight to see what everyone else – as happened so often – simply failed to take heed of.

It did not start as anything remarkable. Ozma was being especially mean, and Toto felt he had done something wrong and so kept away from the Princess. But this did not keep Toto from watching over her, keeping an eye out for her – even if it was at a distance.

And it was at a distance that the little dog first noticed. In truth, he smelled it. An odd odor that began to appear in places around the palace as he followed Ozma. It was faint at first, and Toto was not certain what to make of it. It was not the smell of the cricket or mouse, or any other creature in Oz he knew of. And it was not at all pleasant, especially as it became stronger and more pungent as the day went on. He had caught the first scent of it the morning after Ozma had cast him out of her room, and it had only grown more and more distinct since.

It was halfway through that first day that Toto recognized at least part of what it reminded him of – something rotten, something sour. Nothing specific – it did not smell like bad eggs or meat, for example. It simply smelled bad. But bad was definitely not good if it was in the Emerald Palace, for nothing had *ever* smelled that bad here in all the years he had patrolled the halls and even in the city itself.

What became even more obvious as the stench became more prevalent was that it was not just appearing wherever Ozma was

– it *was* Ozma who smelled this way. Something on Ozma's person was the cause of the bad smell, and the more Toto followed the Princess, the more convinced he was that it was not just something in her clothes – it was the Princess herself that smelled.

Once he recognized where the smell was coming from, the little dog immediately set out to find the palace maid, Jellia Jamb. The pretty little Green Girl was responsible for everything there was in the palace that involved cleaning, and if Ozma was unclean, she would be the one person who might know why.

Only – Jellia was nowhere to be found. Not in the palace nor in the Emerald City itself. And the small dog could find no one to even ask where she might be, either. It was as though the entire palace staff had vanished all around him.

Meanwhile, Ozma had taken to being accompanied by a strange Munchkin lad whom Toto did not know whenever she was in her throne room, where always before it had been Jellia who had stood in service to the Princess. Apparently the strange young man stayed there at all times, even when Ozma was not present. What he did there by himself Toto could not even begin to guess at.

Things were quickly growing very, *very* wrong. And Toto was at a complete loss for how to fix them. The only familiar face the canine could find was the mounted head of the Gump, who was yet another magically enchanted creature hung in one of the great halls of the palace. Periodically, he was moved to new locations because unlike other creatures, he could not move himself. His present placement was in a large room high enough in the palace that he could view the hills and vales of Oz beyond the walls of the Emerald City.

Yet all the Gump could talk about was how he was supposed to have been moved by now and Jillia had not come to find him a new place to be. Of course, this only supported the dog's fear that something had befallen Jillia, but he spared the poor Gump this information. There was no sense in upsetting the poor creature, after all, when he could not move about to help Toto in his search.

Eventually, all Toto's searching just brought him back to Ozma. Everything had begun to change shortly after his return to Oz from wherever it was that Ozma had sent he and Dorothy. Perhaps it had been the same magic that had kept Ozma from bringing Dorothy back, or perhaps Ozma had not been honest about the Magic Picture being broken or the Magic Belt not working in the first place. Either way, everything started and ended with Ozma, and Toto was convinced that whatever answers he needed to find could only be found through her.

Clearly, something was wrong with the Princess. She had not been acting herself, she was keeping company with a strange boy, and she smelled wrong, as well. Not to mention that all the normal people whom she would normally surround herself were gone. She had even sent her Captain General and the rest of her army away for some reason.

And so the third day following Dorothy's disappearance found Toto shadowing the Princess. However, it had not amounted to much. Most of her time was spent in her chambers with the door closed. She had ventured out once to sit in her throne room for a time, but if Toto were honest, it seemed more just to revel in *being* seated upon the throne than anything else. There was no one else there but the odd Munchkin lad, and she barely spoke to him. Then she had simply walked back to her room where she had been the rest of the day.

As has been mentioned, Toto is a dog, and dog's are creatures of action. Sitting and watching a closed door for several hours was *not* what Toto had in mind when he took up this task, and all he found himself doing was grinding his teeth waiting for something – *anything* – to happen.

"They say," came a strange voice the dog did not know, "that if you stay in one place long enough, everything you might ever want to happen – will."

Toto jerked up and looked around, smelling the air experimentally. A low growl echoed from his throat and his fur began to rise in challenge, but there was no one else around.

"Of course," said the voice again, "I have never been able to do it myself." Then the voice *tssked*. "And clearly, neither can you. Well, I suppose we will just have to wait for someone else to try it."

It was just before a great large set of teeth appeared in the air a good two feet above his head that Toto detected the first scent of precisely what he was talking to. A cat. It was not Eureka, nor was it the Glass Cat – who actually did not smell of anything. This was a new creature. There was a new cat in Oz. Or at least, part of one.

The little dog felt the rumble in his throat roll down into his chest as he leaned back, preparing to launch himself at the dancing set of smiling teeth.

"Now this is the reason I never brought dogs into the Land," continued the strangely disembodied mouth. "All you ever want to do is growl and bark and bite. It is bad enough we have actual logs – they have bark enough for me!"

Toto realized where he was, being so close to Ozma's room, and reigned in his growling. "What do you want, cat?" snarled the little dog as quietly as he could manage. "I am very busy at the moment. Go to the kitchen and find some milk, or whatever it is you want. But leave the guarding to someone who knows how to do it."

The toothy mouth split in an even wider smile as it bobbed up and down, the sound of hissing laughter escaping from the invisible throat behind it. "Only a dog could sit doing nothing and call it doing something."

"Cat," growled Toto, "Go. Away."

"But I have already been away," said the disembodied voice, a feline leg suddenly appearing out of thin air, pointing to the presumed right of the creature. "I have also been there," another leg appeared, aimed in a different direction, "and there," a third leg appeared, pointing directly up, "and now I am here." At this, a fourth leg appeared with its digits pointed directly at the ground. "So away really is not where I have not already been." As the creature finished, its legs all folded inward, taking the shape of how a cats legs might appear if it were at rest, only without a body to lay upon the appendages themselves.

Toto gave another quick look to Ozma's door. Cats always annoyed him, but this one in particular was proving impossible to deal with. Every instinct Toto had called for him to launch himself at the cat and drive him away. But he knew also that if he caused a commotion now, Ozma would know he was there.

"What are we watching for, anyway?" asked the partially visible feline. All at once, two bouncing balls appeared along the hallway, rolling through the air towards Ozma's door. One ball turned in midair and Toto saw that they were not really plain balls at all – the one that turned was looking back at him with a distinctly slitted pupil. The balls bouncing through the air were the cat's eyes.

The little dog was beside himself. He was so frustrated he could barely stop from howling. "Stay back from there," he yipped as softly as he could manage.

At this, both eyes did stop and looked back at the small dog. "But why?" asked the voice of the cat, which now appeared to be somewhere near the eyeballs. Just as Toto began to turn to see if the mouth was indeed still where it had been before, the creature's entire tawny-striped head took shape around the bobbing eyes. "To watch, does that not suggest we must see?"

Toto took a deep breath, doing his best to contain his anger. "I am trying to watch without being seen," he explained. All the

Ron Glick - 60

while, a little voice in the dog's mind was applauding himself for his restraint. *Dorothy would be so proud! She did not have to be here to keep me from biting off this cat's head – if that were even possible with this one!*

Without warning, the cat's head made to leap forward, with the creature's full body materializing around him as he came to land on some invisible surface directly in front of Toto's face. The cat's leering grin fairly split the creature's head in half as he said, "Then how so ever shall we find the witch?"

Toto was about to bark a rebuke when the meaning of the words sunk in. "Witch?"

The cat reached out a claw and tapped it sharply into Toto's nose. "Why, is there something wrong with your nose? Can you not smell her?"

"Smell?" Toto asked dumbly.

The cat turned and sauntered a few steps away from the small dog, seemingly walking up an invisible incline as he did so. "Her magic is not working right, or I am sure it would have taken much, much longer to notice. But glamors always begin to fade in time, changing into the opposite of what they are."

"What are you saying?" asked Toto, genuinely intrigued by the cat's words.

"A glamor is all about making something *look* nice, is it not?" yawned the cat, looking back over his shoulder at the dog. "So when it changes, would it not begin to *smell* bad?"

All at once, Toto remembered Glinda's words from shortly before sending Dorothy and himself after the Wizard.

Two prisoners gone. And one a former wicked witch.

The Wizard had not been the only one to go missing from the Emerald City. *Mombi* had, as well. And Mombi was the witch who had once known how to cast magical disguises...

Toto looked past the cat at the Princess' door with new understanding. "That's not Ozma," he gasped. *But is it Mombi? It could be just someone Mombi disguised...*

No. Toto knew that was not true the moment he considered it. He may not have been able to understand *why* people acted the way they did, but it did not mean he did not know *that* they did. He had never dealt with the Wicked Witches overly much – only one in fact – but he had dealt with more than enough people who wanted to take over Oz for their own reasons through the years. And they all wanted to sit upon the Emerald Throne. Not seat someone else there – sit there themselves.

If this person pretending to be Ozma was anyone, it could only be the former Wicked Witch herself. She would want to rule Oz, and what better way than to make herself look like Ozma? Who would challenge her right to rule is she appeared to be the Crown Princess?

Toto took a step toward the cat, who now was splayed out on his side close to the ceiling preening himself. Even at this distance, the little dog could hear the sound of the cat purring. "That is not the Princess behind that door. It is the witch, Mombi."

The cat opened one of its eyes. "You do not say? Well, we did know she was about somewhere."

Armed with this new information, Toto prepared himself to charge the door.

"Of course," spoke up the cat, "knowing this Ozma person is not really Ozma means one does not know where Ozma actually is." The cat raised his head and looked down at Toto attentively. "Is that important, at all?"

The canine stopped himself in mid-step. The cat was right. He needed to find where Ozma was first. Only then could he go against the imposter.

And Jellia. And all the rest of the palace staff whom he could not find. This had become more than just working out why Ozma was acting strange – this had suddenly become a rescue mission.

Another thought crossed the small dog's mind at that moment. He actually owed a cat – a *cat* – for helping him reason out this puzzle. There could be no greater shame than having to admit that it had been this strange feline who had literally appeared out of nowhere to help him. He was a *dog*, by every bone he had ever buried. But – he was also an *honorable* dog. And that meant he owed the cat at the very least an apology.

Yet when he looked back to where the cat had last been, Toto found the hall completely empty. No cat, no partial floating body parts. Even the feline's scent was gone. It was if the cat had never been there in the first place.

"Are you really gone, or are you just hiding again?" asked Toto hesitantly, feeling more than a little self-conscious at speaking to empty air. But no answer came back to him.

"Just like a cat," grumbled the dog, taking back his earlier reasoning that he owed the cat any kind of consolation. "Running away when there's actual work to be done."

Memories of all the times when Eureka had sat idly by while something important was happening all around her flashed through his mind, but he forcefully willed himself to set aside his old grudges against cats in general. All of Oz was in danger if Mombi had managed to steal the throne. And apparently, he was the only one who was able to do anything about it.

Once again, it is up to the dog to do everyone else's job for them...

Chapter 6

Courting a Queen

The White Rabbit raced along the walkway, his pocket watch clanging loudly upon the outside of his armor. The whole matter of how his watch had come to be upon the outside of the metal plate had been difficult enough to get his mind around, but its constant rattling against the metal he was certain was bound to drive him madder than the Hatter. And if he could not run away from madness, what point was there to hurry in a direction leading away from the King of Hearts' house?

Well, it had *been* the King of Heart's house, before the King had thrown down his crown and rode off to fight the Giant. Now it was the Hatter King's residence, from where that King ruled over the Land. Of course, if the King of Hearts returned to the house, there was no telling whose house it would be then. Which was another reason why the Rabbit's plans for revolution needed to be accomplished soon, before the King of Hearts gave up looking for him – since the last the Rabbit had seen the King, his majesty had been engaged in trying to skewer the Rabbit himself – and decided to return home.

"That would not do," muttered the Rabbit as he gasped for breath. "No, that would not do at all. How will the revolution happen if the Kings start fighting too soon?"

Well, if all continued as he had left it with the Hatter King, they would not *be* at the King's house much longer. But of course, the Hatter was nothing if not one to change his mind as often as he did his head wear. No, the Rabbit knew he would have to return to the Hatter King at least one more time before he set off to send the King of Hearts into the revolutionary war.

Once the Rabbit had decided that the only way he could possibly continue to serve the Crown in all its myriad forms was to mount a revolution, he had spent some time making sure the Hatter King was willing to take part in his plan. Of course, being a revolutionary meant being secretive, so he could not simply come out and *tell* the King what his plans were. He needed to convince the King to do what needed to be done without mentioning what *actually* needed doing.

With the Hatter King, it was nearly as impossible to reason with him as it was with the Queen of Hearts herself. It was bad enough that that Hare would stand in as the Hatter's Queen whenever he was not trying to be King himself, but the Hatter was a truly demanding King all on his own. He would come up with new orders and commands faster than anyone in his court could fulfill his previous ones. This meant that, more often than not, the Hatter King's court was scattered to the winds acting out the his wishes, while other times the King could not be pinned down himself for wanting to be out and about following his own orders.

In that much, at least, the Hare was a grounding influence. Whenever the Hatter King decided he wanted to race off on one impulse or another, it would be the Hare who would remind him that he needed to stay where he was if he wished to be King. Half the time, this would result in the Hatter throwing down the crown, followed by he and the Hare fighting over it. The other half of the time, it would result in the King pouting, which made approaching him about anything nigh impossible.

However, in order for the Hatter King to take part in the his revolution, the Rabbit needed to convince the King *and* the Hare of the need to actually leave the King of Heart's house. There could be no revolutionary war if all the aspects of the Crown were not involved, after all, and so he needed to get the Hatter King and the Hare to agree on fighting in the war. Yet, as much as the two seemed inseparable in so many ways, the one thing they could rarely do was come to a complete agreement.

Whenever the Rabbit could convince the King to go, the Hatter would remind him to stay. Whenever the Rabbit could convince the Hare of the need to go, the King would find some new thought to distract him from the idea altogether.

The only thing that made the Rabbit's task easier was that the King at least knew there was a civil war in the Land between the various aspects of the Crown. The King of Hearts was at war with the Queen of Hearts, and the Hatter King was at odds with both – mostly just because it seemed the politically correct thing to do while the other King and Queen were not getting along. But at least because there was *another* war about, the Rabbit could use words like "battle" and "fighting" without making the Hatter King and his (sometimes) Queen call for his court martial yet again for treason.

In the end, the Hatter had ended up sending away most of his court on one errand or another, leaving the Rabbit alone with the present Hatter King and Queen. When the Hare complained that no one was there to treat him like a queen, the Rabbit seized on the idea and told them that the reason why was because not enough of his citizens knew the Hatter was wearing the crown. If more people *knew* he was the King, there would be more to act as their servants.

The Hare leaped at the idea – literally, jumping nearly a foot up in the air at the notion. For once, he agreed that the King needed to go out to his people and tell them that he was the King – because, after all, he had the crown. The Rabbit added to this by reminding the Hatter that no other King could make such a claim. And just like that, the two had run off to pack for their journey.

Of course, this meant more of them running around the throne room collecting discarded tea cups and other miscellaneous items that the Rabbit could see no genuine use for, but it was better than their not doing anything at all. And as they ran about the room collecting things, it gave the Rabbit the opportunity to tell them *where* they needed to go first. After all, where better to begin making announcements as the King than the place the other King had last been seen?

Both of the usurping royals agreed this was a marvelous idea – yet another miracle that they had agreed on two things back to back. Before he could jinx it further, the White Rabbit had bowed and left, assuring both the Hatter King and Queen that he would meet them there.

Yet for now, his task was to engage the Queen of Hearts. He had the Hatter King and Queen on their way, and the King of Hearts would be the easiest to lead to the site of the revolutionary war. But the Queen of Hearts... Oh, the Queen. Now she would be the greatest of all the challenges the Rabbit needed to face to make his revolution happen.

So lost was the Rabbit in his plotting and scheming, that he arrived at the outlying hedges of the Queen of Heart's court without even realizing it. A moment of trepidation seized him, making him pause. This was soon replaced by the excitement he always felt at doing what he did so well and he took his first step towards the Queen's castle...

Then stopped.

The White Rabbit's ears slowly laid flat upon his head as the very head itself equally slowly looked behind him to verify what he had just realized. And, true to his fear, it had been just as he thought.

"Oh, this cannot be," whispered the Rabbit, his voice shaking with disbelief. "My oh my, but this will not do. It cannot, *must not* be."

With his mind so twisted with new thoughts and ideas, the Rabbit had completely missed that he had arrived quite suddenly in the Queen's gardens. But one did not enter a Queen's court without first making a grand entrance. No, not at all. But... What had happened to the entrance?!

To reach the Queen's court, one was expected to pass through the hall and then the door at the end of the hall. Regardless how one entered the hall – whether by the many paths that led there or even from the so-called Rabbit Hole (oh, how Alice had mucked that one up by naming it after him), it nevertheless always ended the same: at the entrance to the Queen of Hearts' court.

Only, the Rabbit had not come through the hall. In fact, he had not even seen it in passing through the door at the end of the hall – mostly because the door, much like the hall itself, had not *been* there to see.

The Rabbit's nose twitched and his whiskers shivered. He turned himself around again and again, looking for some sign that he was not truly where he was – because surely that could have been the only answer. Yet no matter how many times he turned in a circle, he was still exactly where he was – and that was at the edge of the Queen of Hearts' court. Or more specifically, at the edge of her court gardens.

"Oh dear. Oh dear, oh dear, oh dear." The White Rabbit could think of nothing else to say. He could not in fact *think* at all. One could not enter a room without a door, so how could he possibly have entered the Queen's court without one?

When the Rabbit's mind *did* start working, his hands went promptly to his neck. "My head!" he gasped, looking about in desperation. If anyone had seen him enter the Queen's court without making his expected entrance, his revolution would be short lived indeed! The Queen of Hearts was notorious for calling, "Off with his head!" over the slightest provocation. And he could not imagine she would take lightly to the idea of the Rabbit breaking such a steadfast rule as this one.

Thankfully, no one was about and the Rabbit lowered his hands. His right hand reached nervously for his watch, but found that it was not hanging outside his metal vest any longer. His first thought was that the watch must have found its way back into his breast pocket, but that idea vanished when he found the end of the watch's chain still hanging freely from below the chest plate – sans the watch itself.

The watch had broken free and fallen away at some point during the Rabbit's mad dash here. He was amazed that he had not noticed it, for it would have been the end of the deafening and oh-so-irritating banging sound that had accompanied him the entire way. And yet – here he was, with no more a watch than an entrance into the Queen's court.

"Well, if I'm late," mused the Rabbit, "at least I shall have an excuse this time." Not that excuses warranted pardons when it came to the Queen, of course.

Burying his concerns over the vanished entrance, the Rabbit decided his only course lay ahead of him. He still needed to convince the Queen to take part in the revolution – for what else could a loyal subject do?

With a skip that was at best half-hearted, the Rabbit began to run through the opening in the hedges and into the garden proper. He cast his eyes about as he moved, looking for the royal entourage that more frequently than not preceded the Queen of Hearts wherever she went. He personally knew that her escort had diminished in number ever since the the civil war had begun – with half the guards and citizens going to serve in the King's court – but it was still usually a boisterous enough affair to spot at a distance.

There were no trumpets or calls echoing in the gardens this day however, and so the Rabbit presumed the court must be gathered inside the Queen's castle. This presumption led him as he began to run at an ever faster rate, and in doing so nearly ran past the object of his search entirely. He did, actually, run past her and had to double back once his mind had acknowledged what his eyes had seen.

The Queen of Hearts was seated on a stone bench in between two hedge rows, with her only accompaniment being the Knave of Hearts, who stood dejected to her side. Upon seeing the

Rabbit – the second time, for he had missed the Rabbit's first passing as the Rabbit himself had almost missed their standing there altogether – the Knave made an elaborate bow, yet the ever present smile that was always a part of his composure was at best a halfway measure.

"My Queen," blurted the Rabbit, realizing only then how out of breath he was, "I have been searching for you."

"You very nearly failed," scolded the Queen, swishing in the Rabbit's general direction with her hand.

"And yet, here I am," rebutted the Rabbit, standing as tall as his nerves and pride would allow.

"Oh, Rabbit, you have come at a most dire time," continued the Queen, countering her stress of concern by yawning. "There seems some question as to what loyalty to one's Queen truly means. And I can think of none better than you to demonstrate."

The White Rabbit's eyelids batted quickly as he tried to think fast. *Has she uncovered my revolution already?* The mere thought sent his heart racing.

"Wh- what can *I* do or say, your highness? I am but a loyal servant of the Crown."

"It would seem," said the Queen, waving a previously unseen piece of paper in the air, "that the Knave has decided that a Queen must have a King, and he has pronounced that in his loyalty, he would ask my hand to stand as my King."

The Rabbit turned to the Knave for confirmation. The Knave in return only stared at his shoes as he kicked at some invisible object directly in front of him.

"Is this true?" asked the Rabbit, his thoughts of revolution momentarily shocked from his mind. *Another King?* How could he ever keep all the Kings straight if a third came to be?

"I would not speak against the Queen," pronounced the Knave, "for I would keep my head. But I must say in my defense, if such things are allowed, that there is no proof that I made such an offer. The note she waves about is unsigned, if you will but look."

The Rabbit scrunched his brow. This seemed a common defense for the Knave of Hearts. Whenever he was caught in one bad act or another, a letter would always appear condemning him. Yet it would always be unsigned, and it would always be the first defense the Knave would raise for himself.

"The Queen is at war, good Knave," said the White Rabbit, in as official a capacity as he could. "Would you have a wedding before the King's head is even removed? And what crown would you wear, if not the one upon the King's brow even now?"

Of course, the Rabbit knew that the King who did wear the crown was not actually the one the Queen had ordered to have his head removed. But to explain his knowledge of this would have gone against his loyalty to the Kings, and so he chose to not elaborate upon this point.

"Then be done with the war," suggested the Knave, showing quite a bit more defiance than was his norm. "Be done with the King, and someone new might step up to be King."

Someone would need be done with two rather than one, first, thought the Rabbit. *Twice the task you think it to be, dear Knave.*

Aloud, the Rabbit said, "I could not agree with you more. The war must be done. And, if I may, Your Majesty," and to this, he turned to the Queen. "the Knave is not wrong. A Queen does need a King. Or, if I may be so bold, *this* Queen needs a King."

The Queen of Hearts sat upright, her face beginning to flush. "Would you command your Queen in what to do, Herald?"

"No, no," sputtered the Rabbit, flashing his hands before him in a sign of submission. "Only that the war has all your subjects at ends and odds, and much more mixed and jumbled than is good. It is what I have seen as I have been about your service."

"Now you would say I am trouble to my servants?"

"It is the *King* who is the trouble," pleaded the Rabbit, falling to his knees in supplication. "The *King*, I say. Which is why he must be done away with, just as the Knave says!"

The Queen's face lessened in color, and she took on a more thoughtful posture. "Yes, I have already ordered the King's head off, and yet none has brought it to me. Do you say he has not given up his head, Rabbit?"

"No, my Queen. This is why we are at war – because the King will not follow your commands." The Rabbit was about to continue, when he remembered where he was supposed to be guiding the Queen. He had been focused too much on his own self-preservation and had almost missed the chance to send the Queen to the site of his revolutionary war.

"But we must remember *why* the King refused your order to have his head off," interjected the White Rabbit cunningly. Or at least, he hoped it was cunning and not instead too forward. He had already spared his head from being removed once already in this conversation, after all. "And that is the Giant. He is the one who *told* the King to not follow your command, and he is the real reason for the war. And he is the one the King even now chases all over the Land as a reason to not have his head off. I would even go so far as to guess that with the Giant no longer a threat to the Land, that the King would no longer be able to refuse to submit to your command, at all."

"So if we could take the Giant's head off," said the Queen, stopping to raise a finger to emphasize her next point, "whom I have also already commanded to have his head off – then the King would come and have his head off, as well?"

"Well, there certainly would be no other excuse for him not to," said the Rabbit.

The Queen nodded her understanding, and then turned her attention once more to the paper in her hand. "And what do we do with the Knave who would seek to be my King? I am of a mind to order his head--"

"Not without a trial," said the Knave in his own defense, "and with no King, there can be no trial. For the King is always the judge of any trial. But of course, if the Queen were to raise someone to King – perhaps even myself, as the letter which I did not write suggests – then there would be someone to oversee the trial, after all."

The Rabbit groaned inwardly. Who knew the Knave of all people had ever had ambitions to rule? He had ever been a supplicant, serving the whims of the court much as he himself did. Though, if truth be told, the Rabbit had long thought that the Knave's elaborate service was a ruse to hide his own misconduct from the eyes of the King and Queen, as his numerous charges over time had demonstrated. Somehow, he had always prevailed once he had called for a trial, which is the only reason he had stayed in the Queen's court, at all.

"If I may, Your Majesty," offered the Rabbit, "I would suggest that the matter of the current King be addressed before the subject of a new King is raised. As the Knave says, you *do* need a King for a trial, and we cannot have another King," *a third King*, the Rabbit inserted to himself, "while we have yet to settle the issue of the first."

The Queen tapped her finger to her lower lip. "I quite agree. We must settle with the King of Hearts. I must admit, I much more like the idea that I simply order the Knave's head off, but I seem to have a list of heads that already have yet to come off, and who is to know how long it would be before the Knave's turn came."

The Queen rose, taking command of the scene. "So it is off to find the heads to whom I am already owed."

The Rabbit and Knave both bowed.

"Yes, my Queen," said the Knave.

The Rabbit, however, had more to add. "My Queen, there is only the issue of where to *find* the King. And I do believe I can be of some help in that."

The Queen raised her chin. "Speak then, Rabbit. Where is my irksome King?"

The Rabbit felt his left lip twitch as he tried to suppress a grin. "As I have gone about your service, it just so happens that I have come upon where the Giant is hiding. And since I know the King is about looking for the Giant, I can lead him there myself."

The Queen smiled wickedly. "I believe I do see your plot, my Herald. You would have me lead the army there to catch the King as he tries for the Giant, and thereby take both at the same time!"

The White Rabbit could not suppress his smile this time, but he bobbed his head to hide that it was for anything more than being praised by his liege. "Yes, my Queen. If you but lead your army to the Giant's hideaway, I can bring the King there and then you can have off with both their heads!"

"Oh, clever, clever," mused the Queen. "And where would this hideaway be?"

At this, the Rabbit stood erect, puffing out his chest. "Why, in the old Wyrds' Castle, my Queen."

I've done it! thought the White Rabbit. *With the Hatter King already marching and the Queen soon to follow, all I need do is lead the King of Hearts to the war. And just like that, the revolution will be over!*

Chapter 7

An Unexpected Obstacle

It was one thing to say something needed doing – but it was not always clear on how such a thing needed to be done. This was the dilemma presently being faced by Alice's group. Glinda and Alasia were both clearly in agreement that they must keep Mombi's castle from being taken by the former Wicked Witch of the North, and yet none of them knew precisely how to accomplish such a feat.

The seven comrades had continued to watch the excavation from the neighboring hilltop until dusk made it too difficult to make out what work was being accomplished. By then, the tower which had been cleared stood well over four times the height of the men working to dig it free, which made it by Glinda's estimate some twenty-five feet clear. By that height, Alasia assured them all, the first window should have been cleared and possibly a second – which could potentially grant anyone with the inclination access to the castle's interior.

Alice, of course, had laughed at the idea. "Would not the rooms be full of dirt, as well?" she had asked.

"That all depends," said Alasia icily, "upon how *fast* the castle was buried, *how* the castle was buried, and with *what* materials. Honestly, child. Think before you speak!"

This had earned Alasia a rebuke from Glinda, but the answer had still largely not been given, though Alice certainly had no intention of asking it again with the nasty witch around. The girl had her own ideas on the subject at any rate, but decided to wait to speak with Glinda alone.

That evening, the group retired to Betsy's small cabin. The little building barely had three rooms – one of which was a common room – and a stable, so to say they found themselves crowded in the interior went without saying. But it was the closest thing to privacy the party could hope for with the army stationed so closely nearby

While traveling about England and France with her father as a girl, Alice had on occasion encountered military men. She knew they had a love for patrols and "keeping watch" over wherever they were stationed, so the idea of being indoors – away from where there voices could be heard by someone unknown in the dark – had seemed a positively brilliant notion. However, it did nothing for settling Alasia, who seemed disagreeable about most everything – and being confined in Betsy's cabin was no exception.

"Did Locasta never tell you how she managed to bury the castle in the first place?" asked Alasia shortly after Betsy had served her company some stew. The old witch only jabbed at the meat and potatoes and seemed not at all interested in actually eating it.

Perhaps Alasia wants to talk now because she does not wish to eat like the rest of us, thought Alice. And come to think of it, even on their journey north, Alice could not recall the old woman actually eating anything. Which made her wonder whether the old witch even needed to eat, or if she did, what it was she preferred to eat in the first place.

Alice shivered at the notion, but when no one else bothered to respond to Alasia's grousing, she offered her own idea – in spite of her earlier commitment to speak to Glinda about it in private.

"I do not believe the castle *was* buried," said Alice softly, following her words with a quick mouthful of stew.

"Of all the ridiculous notions!" scoffed the old witch. "Of course it's buried! What do you think they are doing out there, carving it out of stone as we speak?"

"Alasia!" scolded Glinda. "Mind your tone!" The old woman just scowled, and went back to stabbing at the food in her earthen bowl.

Turning to Alice, Glinda asked, "Why do you say that, dear Alice?" For some reason, Alasia made a grunting noise as Glinda finished, but did not interrupt otherwise.

Alice looked up at the Good Witch. "It is true that the castle is under the ground. But the army is not digging on top of a hill. They are working in a valley. If the castle were buried, there would be a great mound of dirt built up around it." Alice emphasized her words by raising her arms high in the air in the shape of a large round hill. "But since they are in a valley, it would seem that the ground was not brought up to bury the castle, at all. It is too flat for that." The girl brought her hands down to the table to demonstrate a flat area. "I would think that this means the castle fell into the ground, not the other way around."

Glinda's eyes brightened. "Marvelous idea, Alice!" Glinda turned to the old witch. "In answer to your question, I was not present when Locasta hid Mombi's castle. I was told she buried it, but as Alice says, that may not be precise. As I recall, even my Great Book of Records only says that Locasta cast a spell to hide the castle of the Wicked Witch of the North beneath the ground."

As the other witch talked, Alasia actually put a piece of meat in her mouth and began to chew it, seeming to take a considerably longer time than needed to grind the food. "You realize," said Alasia, as her jaw still worked at her meat, "this is perhaps the longest the two of us have spoken about anything since you first... won out against Theysla. This might be a good point to ask a question or two that has always befuddled me."

Glinda cocked her head and narrowed her eyes, clearly not trusting where the old witch's line of inquiry was leading. And honestly, even Alice doubted it would glean anything constructive. Likely, thought the girl, it was just an excuse to begin another argument, as Alasia was wont to do.

"I do not know if now is the time, Alasia," said the Good Witch cautiously. "There is certainly much and more you do not know, and we only have this one evening to plan for how to keep the castle over yonder hill from Mombi. But I concede this is a rare moment, and if it will ease you in some small way, I will agree to answer one of your questions now, and will make myself and my Book of Records at your disposal should this affair end with good behavior upon your part. Is this acceptable?"

The former Wicked Witch of the East sneered broadly, and made to swallow her food. "One is all I need for now, as it might answer my earlier question at the same time." Pausing dramatically, the old witch leaned forward and asked in a gravelly, ominous voice, "Where did Locasta come from?"

Glinda blinked and sat back. She began to open her mouth, but Alasia held up one crooked finger to halt her.

"Do not let my question be wasted," said the old woman. "I already know where *you* came from." Alice did not miss the emphasis in Alasia's words, but was not given a chance to ask its meaning before the old witch continued.

"But before we Wyrds came to Oz, there had never been a witch here. The only magic that existed here before us witches was faery magic. This was one reason why no one in Oz knew how to defeat us, because our magic was unknown to the citizens of Oz. It was the same kind of idea that the Wizard used, only his was a trick. He made us all think that he, too, possessed a kind of magic none of us knew how to overcome, which was why he was allowed to take over the Royal Seat of Oz without a fight. And this is why we witches never moved against him. Well, partially. But that is another matter.

"You see, I can account for every witch in Oz, except for Locasta. She came out of nowhere, it would seem, and took Mombi out of power. And Mombi was no weak witch. She might be the youngest of us, but her magic was quite powerful. Yet, not only did Locasta defeat her, but she buried or sunk or whatever she did to put Mombi's seat of power under the ground. Only since then, Locasta has shown no great magic, at all. She barely qualifies as a witch at all these days."

Alasia coughed to clear her throat. "So I ask again – where did such a suddenly powerful witch come from, knowing that she does not seem to really possess near the magic needed to overcome one of the Wicked Witches in the first place?"

Alice looked to Glinda and saw that the Good Witch had calmly reclined in her chair, waiting patiently for Alasia to finish. "The only answer I can give you," said Glinda, "is that she came from somewhere outside of Oz. Just like you and your sisters did. My Great Book of Records only records all that happens within Oz itself, and so where Locasta came from before she entered this realm is a mystery to me, as well as everyone else.

"As for her magic, she certainly had more when she came here, and it has declined over time. Or at least, it certainly appears to have. I cannot say why, nor have I asked. Locasta may have earned the title of being a Good Witch, but she is quite secretive about herself. I have never had a reason to pry, and so I have left it as it is."

"I suppose that is one of your *good* traits that you picked up, is it?" grumbled Alasia, throwing herself back into her chair with her arms crossed.

Much like a spoiled child, observed Alice.

"I have done as I have said I would," said Glinda. "And perhaps a bit more by answering your unasked question about Locasta's magic, as well. May we now focus on the task at hand?"

Alasia waved her hand dismissively. With leave to continue, however rudely delivered, Glinda must have felt that it was time to begin discussing what plan could be made. And so, setting aside her own spoon, she rose to stand before the small group clustered together in what felt to Alice like an even smaller room.

"First, let me say for everyone's benefit what we know, so we can plan for what we do not." Glinda looked about to see if anyone had any other suggestion, but when everyone – except for Alasia, who continued to pout in her chair – looked upon her for her next words, the Good Witch continued.

"The army cannot be seen as our friends, for they are here upon Ozma's commands. Even if we know that the Ozma who gave them their orders is truly Mombi in disguise, we cannot rely upon their believing us. They also have Tik-Tok and many of the local Gillikin farmers pressed into service, which gives us quite a few who would be in our way should they stand and defend Ozma's orders.

"Is there anything I am forgetting?" Again, the Good Witch paused for responses.

"We *could* wait for Tik-Tok to wind down," suggested Hank the Mule. "We would have one less to worry about then."

"Yes, but you know that Omby Amby knows how to wind him," inserted Betsy, "for he has been about the Emerald Palace for as long as we have been in Oz."

"Maybe he will forget?" offered the Mule. "He *does* have a lot of people all around him down there."

"Which raises the point," offered Nick Chopper, "that even without Tik-Tok, there are too many to fight through. Even for me." To emphasize his words, he gripped his ax firmly.

"Then it would seem to me," suggested Alice, "that the goal must be to approach the castle without being seen."

"But what would that accomplish?" asked Alasia spitefully. "Getting *to* the castle ourselves is not the point. Keeping *Mombi* from getting there *is*."

"I would think," said Alice, "that we could better decide what to do *with* the castle if we were able to see the castle up close. And besides, if it is as you say and there is a window, that could also let us know if anyone can yet get in the castle."

"So what you are saying, Alice," interrupted Glinda, "is that we do not know enough as yet to make a plan without first seeing the castle for ourselves?"

"It would seem the most practical thing," agreed the Oxford girl. "None of us know how the castle was put in the ground, so there is no way to put it back. It would seem to me the only way to keep Mombi away is if we are there at the castle to do it ourselves. And we must need do it without the army learning of our plans."

"And it must be done unseen," added the Tin Woodsman. "Which must mean we do it at night."

Several echoing voices of consent rose at this, with more than one acknowledging it should be done this very night.

"If I may suggest something," offered Betsy. "If there is a chance to enter the castle, might it not be a good idea to bring along someone who knows about going underground? The Shaggy Man and his brother – especially his brother – would be the ones to ask about something like that. They have been working their mines for years."

"Do you know where we can find them, Betsy?" asked Glinda.

"Hank knows," the girl said, running her hand along the mule's broad side. "He takes supplies to them."

"How soon could you run there and be back?" asked Nick.

"Not fast enough," admitted the mule. "I could not be back before midday tomorrow, even without bringing back two who were walking."

"If only *I* knew where this place was," interjected the Sawhorse in his woodsy voice. "I am sure *I* could be there and back in time."

Glinda sighed. "An excellent suggestion, Betsy, but one that we do not have time to employ. We will have to make due with whom we have gathered."

"What about Locasta then?" spoke up Alasia. "Would it not be prudent to have the local witch involved in this? She would even know how to bury the cursed thing again."

"Alas, Locasta has not responded to my summons," answered Glinda. "I have been sending for her in the way Good Witches can with each other since we first set out for Gillikin Country. But Locasta has not answered. And her own demesne is too far even for Sawhorse to travel there and back by sunrise. And that is assuming she is even at home."

When no one else had any further suggestions, Glinda decided that there was no better time to act than the moment at hand. Night had fallen quite some time ago, and there was a good chance that the army would be asleep. Glinda called for a vote, and all agreed – save for Alasia, who thought the plan could wait another day to bring the others who had been suggested, especially the Good Witch of the North herself. But the concern of how much more could be uncovered if given another day was too urgent a concern, and Alasia's objections were disregarded.

It did not escape Alice's notice that the old witch did not take the matter lightly, either. There was an anger brewing inside the witch, and the girl from Oxford did not need any magic to know it would not likely bode well for their enterprise.

Alice did remind the Good Witch that there would likely be guards, but Glinda only laughed – with the army of Oz, it was always the privates who were given such tasks, the younger witch explained, and she had not seen any privates milling about the workers. And if there had been, there could only have been a few, as there were never more than two or three privates in the army at any one time.

"So long as we are careful, we should be able to avoid a few who might be guarding," smiled Glinda.

And so the group set out from Betsy's cabin and headed for the hill overlooking the excavation site. Alice held back, feeling the need to keep an eye on Alasia. Though the old witch had agreed to help them keep this castle from Mombi, there was still a part of her that did not trust the old woman. Especially since this expedition was one which the former Wicked Witch had actually been the only dissenting vote on.

The Oxford girl was quite surprised however at exactly how silent the valley beyond the hill was. Where she expected to see camps and fires scattered all about, there was actually only one large fire – and this one actually on the far side of the dig site. There was nothing save the stars and moon – only a sliver in the sky – to provide any light to the scene below. The looming tower was at best only a darker patch against the lighter soil in the distance. Had the group not known what to look for, they might not have seen it at all.

Without any further words, Glinda permitted the Sawhorse and Hank to lead the way, allowing their four-hooved steadfastness to break their path. Besides, if there were any threats about, Hank was the most likely of all present to smell it.

But there was no threat for the group as they descended to the valley floor. No guards came out of the dark to challenge them, and nothing more than a few dug trenches presented any kind of obstacle to their journey. For Alice, it had seemed a nerve-wracking ordeal to walk through the dark, waiting to be discovered. So much so that when they did finally reach the wall of the tower without incident, she found herself letting loose her breath. She had not even realized she had been holding it in.

In total, the tower stood some thirty feet overhead by Alice's best guess, the looming shadow that blocked out the starry sky being her only guide. Like its twin in the east, this castle's stone was a dark color that seemed to absorb all light around, making the edifice fairly blend in with the dark of night. The circumference of the tower was perhaps a hundred feet, judging by the width at its base.

Alice found it remarkable as she ran her hand along the stone how it lacked any signs of having been buried whatsoever. It was as if the men working here had cleaned it as they unburied it, for there were no clusters of dirt nor clotted earth clinging to the exterior walls. *Most peculiar*, thought the girl.

"There," whispered Alasia after several minutes of walking about the base. When the Oxford girl looked, she could see the elderly woman pointing upwards at a point on the wall. As the group gathered around her, the old witch continued. "The window is there, some ten, maybe fifteen feet up. I cannot see how we will reach it without a ladder. Look about--"

"Oh, there's no need for that," spoke up Alice. Without waiting for a response, the girl closed her eyes and focused on what it felt like to fall upwards. This was how she had learned to trigger the magic that had lain dormant in her body since she was a child in Wonderland, and in the barest moment, she did indeed feel as though she were falling straight up into the night sky. When she opened her eyes, she found she was near of a height with the tower, her companions standing at barely above her shin.

"How did she--" started the witch, then fell silent. Alice could imagine the glower that must have come upon the old witch's face. Alasia had not yet known how Alice's magic worked – and it must have caught the old witch off guard.

The Oxford girl knelt down and placed her left hand open-faced upon the ground. "I can lift whoever would like to look at the window," she offered.

"If no one objects," spoke up Nick Chopper, "I shall go first. If there is danger, I would be best suited to face it, after all." The Tin Woodsman gripped his ax meaningfully. "And besides, if there is any digging to be done, I am also the only one with a tool that could be used, though I do so hope I am not forced to soil the shine upon my blade."

None argued the point, and so Alice raised Nick to the place where Alasia had indicated the window should be. True to the old witch's words, once Alice looked closely at the side of the wall, she could make out a darker patch against the stone that could only have been the window. Holding Nick back a moment, she pushed at the darker area with her right forefinger, testing for any resistance. Only emptiness met her exploration, however.

"There does not appear to be any dirt blocking the window," whispered the tall girl to the metal man in the palm of her hand. A sudden image of holding a toy tin soldier flashed into her mind, and she quickly covered her mouth with her other hand to keep from giggling.

"Then raise me up and we shall see how deeply the window is clear," the woodsman whispered back, both of his hands gripping tightly to the ax handle.

Alice raised Nick to the window and the tin man leaped effortlessly into the castle. Alice was amazed that there was not a loud crash to echo the metal man's landing, but somehow the stone seemed to absorb the sound. Yet the dark portal did not keep all sound hidden.

The tin man had been inside the castle for barely a minute when a sudden, sickly green light began to glow from inside. Alice heard Nick call out in surprise and quickly lowered herself to look into the room beyond the window frame, which was now highlighted against the side of the tower.

"Well, if it isn't my fine Tin Man," came a cackling voice from inside the castle. "The rusty old man who took over my kingdom. The Winkies never did have much wisdom scattered about the lot of them."

Alice's eye reached the window just as a silhouetted form stepped out of the shadows, holding a broom in hand with the bristles aimed upward as she came. And it was the bristles themselves which were the source of the eerie green light. They were not on fire, so much as the broom simply appeared to glow in the darkness.

All at once, the woman moved enough that the girl could make out her features, and she gasped as she recognized her. In fact, if it were not for the small detail that she knew Alasia was below, she might have mistaken this new arrival for the former Wicked Witch of the East. She had, after all, been disguised to *look* like Alasia by Mombi. But armed with that knowledge, there was no mistaking who had appeared out of the dark to confront Nick Chopper.

"If you wish to go any further without my leave," said Fenstel, holding her broom forward as though it were a weapon, "you will find your efforts a failure!"

Chapter 8

Escape From the Looking Glass

Dorothy sat down heavily in the stuffed chair yet again. Lifting, sorting and reading through volumes of books was an exhausting task. She simply could not understand how people took such joy in it, even took up jobs researching one thing after another. Her friend the Wogglebug back in Oz could spend weeks at a time shuttered away within the Emerald City's library, and the Wizard himself was known for taking days at a time to do just that. Dorothy had spent barely a day at it herself, and she was nearly ready to forego ever admitting she knew how to read ever again.

"Wizard, I do not believe there is anything here," complained the girl.

"Tsk, tsk," came the old man's voice from across the room. "Surely you have not examined every book there?"

The Wizard had tasked her with searching for anything to do with the the Wyrds, their spell or cats in general. She had to admit that this library contained a great deal of information, but not any of it was useful. It all had nonsense subjects and even more senseless content. It was almost as if the library deliberately wanted to make sure she went the furthest away from the topics she was searching for as possible.

Meanwhile, the Wizard had managed to locate a mirror in one of the other rooms of the castle in Wonderland which could be moved. He had paired it with the mirror through which Dorothy had contacted him, while she had propped open the book that apparently had been Mombi's own records. With this elaborate setup, the old man was able to read the book without having it physically in his presence, reading its reflection in the mirror on his own side. Dorothy had to constantly stop her own searching to turn a page whenever the Wizard required – forward if needed, or back again to re-read something earlier – but at least it gave her small breaks in trying to make sense of why anyone would write entire books about the shade of buttermilk or the migrating patterns of dust particles. The most outrageous series of books she had discovered was a nine volume set discussing the philosophical reasons for writing a nine volume set of books.

In Dorothy's mind, the only logical place to find the Wyrd's spell was in Mombi's own book. She saw no purpose in searching all these other books from Fenstel's library. After all, if Mombi's book contained the Jabberwock story, why would it also not contain the spell which had made it real? Yet so far, no matter how many pages Dorothy turned in Mombi's book, the Wizard could find nothing describing the spell whatsoever.

"Isn't it possible that the witches didn't write anything down, Wizard?" yawned Dorothy. "Or perhaps it was something they took with them? Fenstel did say that they needed to be somewhere away from the castles – would it not make sense that they would take the spell with them?"

The Wizard's voice was silent for a moment. "That is possible," agreed to old man. "I just fear that if we accept that conclusion and you leave the castle you are in, if the answer *does* prove to be there, we might not be able to get back to it."

"Wizard," said Dorothy, casting her eyes helplessly about the room, "I could search here for a year and not have read all that is here. Did you not say we had little time?"

An audible sigh came from behind the glass. "Dorothy, please come to the mirror."

With a deep sigh of her own, Dorthy heaved herself from the chair and walked over to the mirror. Once in line with the glass, she could see the Wizard as he was seated on the other side, leaning upon his cane as he supported the awkward position of reading the book through the mystical device. He was sitting askew of his chair now in order to face the mirror, since his reading had only been possible with his back to it.

"My dear girl," began the Wizard. "You make a true point. And, I fear, I am at a loss as to whether to continue along this vein, and if so, for how much longer we dare. None of us know what event will lead to the destruction of Wonderland, or even whether it will simply fade away or end without any forewarning at all. So in that, you are correct – time is limited. And it is all the more perplexing in not knowing precisely how long we actually have.

"But you must understand. Should we determine to move on, we are no better off than we are now. We still know nothing of how the magic was cast, only the tool by which it was done. You have the Jabberwock story, but no matter how often I read it, or any of the other notes Mombi has committed in these pages, I am no closer to learning how it was done, or – more closely to our own goal here – how to *undo* it."

Dorothy thought about this for a moment. "Then we need to ask Mombi."

"Dorothy, if it were a simple matter of asking Mombi how to undo her spell, I could have stayed in Oz and never come to Wonderland."

"Ozma told me that Glinda has a stone which can make Mombi tell the truth," offered the girl. "She used it once before on Mombi, back when they needed to know that Ozma was really Tip."

"And I suppose you have a plan for *finding* Mombi to use it?"

Dorothy felt her face flush. "I don't have all the answers, Wizard," she retorted. "But I *can* say we are not learning anything here. And besides that, my head hurts!"

The old man closed his eyes and rapped lightly on his forehead with his knuckles. "Oh, I do often forget that not everyone can read so much and not suffer," he confessed.

Looking up again, he smiled. "You are right, of course. I have read most of this book by now, and read several passages so many times I have lost count. You have not learned anything, and it is as you say – it could take far longer than we have to search that library. I regret what we may lose, but you are only one girl – and a girl who cannot be expected to stay and read for days and days as I or others of my learned caste can do."

The Wizard stood up, stretching his back as he did, his face demonstrating the pain sitting for so long had created in his rheumatic bones. "I think it *is* time that you return back through the looking glass in Oxford and come back to Wonderland. Bring the book, and I shall see if there is anything more I can learn while I wait for you."

Dorothy would have leaped out and hugged the Wizard if he had been standing in front of her, she was so giddy. *No more reading!*

"I will gather up some things and be on my way. See you soon, Wizard."

The Wizard waved a half-hearted farewell, and Dorothy rubbed the side of the mirror as Fenstel had instructed her to end the magic. *If only Fenstel's mirrors could send objects through like the one in Alice's Oxford can, and I could be with the Wizard even now.* But Fenstel had been quite clear on that – her power was over *seeing* things, not sending them. That was a power that only Alasia had, somehow tied to making things unseen by sending them elsewhere. Whether she could do so through a mirror or not was something even the former Wicked Witch of the West did not know of her sister.

And so, the only way out of this Looking Glass World was through the mirror in the original sitting room where Dorothy had first arrived. Of course, it also meant navigating back *to* the house, using the strange, backwards movement that she had gained some small control over in order to reach the witch's castle.

Dorothy picked up the book and looked about for something she could use as a sack. She finally decided to use a velvet-like material lying beside the mirror – large enough that she could imagine it might have at one time served as a covering for the glass – and cut away a portion of it with one of the mirror shards lying on the ground. From this, she fashioned a satchel in which she put the book and the hand-held frame that Fenstel had requested. She looked about the room one last time to make certain she was not forgetting anything, then tied up the satchel, tossed it over her shoulder and headed downstairs.

The girl knew from her time in the castle that the rules of the world beyond its walls did not work here. But once she crossed the threshold to the outside, she would once again need to try walking in the opposite direction of where she wished to go. She had managed it well enough in getting to the castle, but she had more than a small amount of lingering doubt that she would be equally successful a second time – especially with the finer points of moving about the inside of the house where she needed to go.

Arriving at the front door, Dorothy took a deep breath, and pulled at the large wooden barrier. The door swung easily inward, exposing the outside world with its snow covered fields to her gaze. She found it interesting that though she had detected no new snow falling while she had worked within the castle – at least not any visible through the library's window – there were no footsteps in the snow approaching the castle. Somehow in arriving, she had left no trail of where she had been.

The girl was not entirely sure whether to feel concern at that observation or not.

In the distance, Dorothy could see the pleasant two story structure that would be the house where she had first entered this land, and would now be her target to reach. Only, she would have to focus on *not* reaching it if she ever intended to do so.

As she stood at the doorway deciding how to begin – for certainly there would be a dividing line between where the backwards effects of this world would take over from the more natural movements within the castle – the girl could see some kind of movement along the ground close to the house in the distance. Whatever it was caused snow to be thrown upwards over and again, though it was all too far away to make out clearly.

Dorothy shrugged. *Might as well get started*, she told herself. And she did.

The Kansas girl took her first step out the door, but nothing immediate happened, so she took a second – and suddenly found herself standing alongside the wall of the castle. She turned and looked about, trying to navigate where she had moved to. As she turned, she caught sight of the door and realized though she had effectively stepped forward, she had instead moved back a short distance from the entryway along the outside of the building.

Well, that makes sense – sort of. I could not very well have gone back into the castle if the castle does not follow these backwards rules.

Convinced she was now fully under the sway of the Looking Glass World, Dorothy glanced over her shoulder to gauge the direction the house lay in, then deliberately walked in the opposite direction – which in this case, would normally have sent her walking into the castle's wall. Yet, just as Dorothy had predicted, she instead found herself further away from the wall instead.

Emboldened, Dorothy set out walking – trying to set her mind toward getting back to the castle, while each step actually took her further and further from the edifice.

The girl felt pride in her ability to adapt to this world so easily. She credited all her adventures in faery realms over the years. Though none had ever required her to rethink how she moved about, they nevertheless made her thoughts about what was considered real to be somewhat more elastic, giving her the capacity to readily accept the need to look at things from a different angle in order to solve whatever problem presented itself.

Dorothy was so involved in applauding her own talents, however, that when she came to an abrupt halt, she found herself stumbling and falling to the ground instead of adapting to the sudden change. Turning about and looking up from the snow, she found herself staring up at an old man mounted upon a white steed with a very long lance aimed down at her. His armor looked positively ancient, like a knight might wear on a field of battle. The only color of note about him was the red color of his lance.

"Be you the waif who did intrude upon yonder castle?" demanded the man on his horse.

"I--" Dorothy was confused, and took a moment to look over her shoulder toward the witch's castle. It was indeed some distance away now, but not as far as she remembered it being when she had first encountered it. She had somehow been stopped midway between the castle and house.

"She is indeed," said a woman's voice, and Dorothy caught sight of the Red Queen approaching. As before, she held her dress above the snow, yet the powdery substance still parted about her feet as though the dress were actually dragging along the ground. "She chose not to go there right after she suggested traveling there to me in person."

"I did go there," confessed Dorothy. The girl was becoming uncomfortably aware that she was still sitting in the snow, and she made to lift herself up. The knight, however, had other ideas, as his horse took a step closer, bringing the point of the spear closer, as well.

"Do you confess then that you defied my decree?" asked the Queen, coming to a stop beside Dorothy. The girl found it most embarrassing, since she could now see up the Queen's dress, though the royal lady seemed to take no notice. And besides, there were such an abundance of undergarments, it was not as if she were exposed, at all, so Dorothy supposed the woman would not really have a reason to be self-conscious.

"What decree?" asked Dorothy. "All I said was that I went to the castle."

"So you do confess?" asked the Queen again.

"Your Majesty," sighed Dorothy, "I am confused. How is saying I went to the castle breaking one of your rules?"

"The Queen did say you could go to the castle, and yet you chose to not go there," interjected the knight. "If you are to go about and not do things of which you have been given leave to do, then there really is no order, at all."

Dorothy struggled with that for a moment. She recalled that more than just direction was backwards in this place. The Red King and Queen had also had a peculiar way of talking backwards, as well. She reflected back on her talk with the Red Queen before she had gone off to the castle – in truth, the Queen had not actually told her to stay or not to stay. But she *had* told her that she could do as she wished – which in this instance was to go to the castle. Only in this backwards place.. and then she puzzled it out.

"You said I could do as I wished, but here that must mean I could not do that. You say you gave me permission to *go*, but that was actually your way of telling me to *stay*," reasoned Dorothy.

"She confesses!" cried the Queen, looking about her. Her manner suggested she were speaking to a large assembly, but there was only Dorothy, the knight and herself present. "The war is over! Everyone can go back home!"

The knight raised his lance, and trotted off without further comment.

"I'm... Can I get up now?" managed Dorothy.

"Of course, of course," responded the Queen, reaching down to help the girl stand. "If you would stay on the ground, it would be as if you were standing all the more, and we cannot have that, can we?"

"So am I still in trouble for leaving? Or not staying, or whatever it is I did wrong?"

"Now what would be the point in that?" asked the Queen, as she began to walk away from Alice. "You confessed and are clearly guilty, so you could only be pardoned. It was all we could do."

Dorothy closed her eyes and shook her head. *The sooner I am away from this place...*

Without thinking, Dorothy started to follow the Queen, since she appeared to be moving toward the house, and found herself stumbling backwards into a trench dug in the snow. *I am truly getting tired of falling down in this snow*, she groused inwardly.

Only then did Dorothy hear the cry of a small child. Sitting up, she noticed a small girl lying in front of her, tears streaming down her cheeks and a shovel lying to her side. For all appearances, the girl had been clearing a path in the snow – which now made sense to Dorothy as to what had been causing the snow to fly up in the distance – and the larger girl had stumbled back over her by walking the wrong way.

"Oh, I am so sorry," said Dorothy, leaning over and picking up the little girl. Carefully, she balanced the small girl on her hip while securing her satchel under her other arm. "There, there, no need to cry."

"My word," came another familiar voice. "She has captured a pawn!"

Dorothy whirled about to see the Red King standing aghast behind her. He stood in the path the small girl had already cleared and behind him and slightly closer to the house, the Kansas girl could see the Red Queen approaching as well. But this time there was no need for her to hold her dress up, since her own path was also cleared.

It was then that Dorothy could see a larger pattern emerging as she looked out across the field – there were several children moving about shoveling paths, but they were not just walkways. Dorothy was close to the intersection of two lines, which clearly were the edges of large squares – one being cleared of snow, while its neighbor was being left alone. The Kansas girl could imagine that if seen from above, the children's pattern would look like a large grid – creating a clear and obvious checkerboard pattern. The children were clearing a board for chess...

"My child!" called the Red Queen. "Please, do not take my child!"

Then it made even more sense – by picking up the girl, Dorothy had made a simple chess move: she had captured a pawn. The Wizard had taught her the game, and though she was not really very good at it, she knew enough to recognize the significance of what she had done. It was precisely as the King said. To these pieces-made-live, the pawns were the children of the King and Queen, which meant what she was really doing was capturing their child.

As Dorothy stood still reasoning it out, the Red Queen bridged the distance between them. "Oh please, do not take my child! It would be as if she never existed, and she could never grow to be Queen!"

The Kansas girl seized upon an idea. "I will spare the... pawn," she said, "if you will but lead me to the library in yonder building. I mean, if you will *not* but lead me there."

"If this is what must be done to be rid of you, then it shall be precisely as you say," nodded the Queen, "for to do otherwise would be to never see you again, and that would be the lesser of things to worry about."

Taking that for agreement, Dorothy set the child down, who rushed immediately to the Red King and disappeared beneath his robes.

The Kansas girl began to turn, but found the Red Queen gripping her arm before she could complete the task. "Let us be untimely," she said, and Dorothy found herself running beside the Queen. The girl could not even remember beginning to run, much less walking, yet she was nevertheless managing to keep pace with the royal as the Red Queen moved at an ever-increasing pace. However, no matter how fast the two ran, Dorothy realized they actually were not moving, at all. In fact, they appeared to be running in place!

After several minutes, the Queen stopped abruptly, and Dorothy's fears were confirmed: they had not moved from where they had started. The Queen appeared quite out of breath, though, and the Kansas girl found herself equally ragged. "I thought..." gasped the girl.

"Well, are you not going to leave?" asked the Queen.

"But we did not go anywhere!" retorted Dorothy.

"Would you question the Queen?" called the King. "I would really like to know, because it would be better than anything I could say, and that is a certainty."

The Red Queen only pointed behind Dorothy, a stern look upon her face. The girl turned to see what the Queen was pointing at – and suddenly found herself inside the house, and facing the very mirror that she had been trying to reach all along.

Quickly, Dorothy turned back to look at the Queen, but all evidence of ever being outside had also vanished.

I had better leave this madhouse while I can, thought the girl. Positioning herself with her back to the mirror, Dorothy did not waste any time in thought. Reason did not work here, and if she paused to think, she might find herself back outside again. Or worse. She took a run and leaped toward the wall on the far side of the room.

And just like that, Dorothy found herself falling from the mantle and onto the carpeted floor of the room. She felt a sharp pain in her side, and realized she had landed upon the satchel, the book's edge digging into her ribs. It took her a moment to catch her breath, but after that, all she could think to do was get up to discover which side of the mirror she had landed on.

The easiest way would just be to walk, reasoned Dorothy, and so she did. She took two firm steps, and when she found that she moved toward rather than away from where she headed, she let out a *yippee!* She had never been so happy to take two steps in her entire life!

But the girl knew she had no time to waste in her exhilaration and made a dash for the doorway and out into the hall beyond. All she could think about was finding her way back to the Rabbit's Hole to get back into Wonderland without delay.

What Dorothy did not see in her rush to leave, however, was the shadow that hovered near the drapes in the room. Its head cocked sideways for a moment, as though thinking about what it had just seen. Then, planting its hands firmly upon its hips, it gave a clear nod of decision. And without another moment's hesitation, it flew out the window into the darkened night sky.

It only took the shadow a moment to get its bearings before it set out on its path, following the stars in the sky – second to the right, and straight on till morning...

Chapter 9

The White Rabbit Triumphant

The one thing that any researcher rarely admitted – whether they be of the sciences or theologies of the world – was that facts sometimes were impossible to discover. They could not, for it would be an admission that their pursuits in life could potentially have no real purpose. None whatsoever. No, a dedicated researcher would always continue looking upon the fundamental belief that whatever it was for which he searched *did* exist, if only he looked far and wide enough to find it. But far more often than any researcher would care to openly admit is that facts supporting their reason for searching did not – nor could they even ever – always actually exist.

And this was the dilemma in which Oscar Zoroaster Phadrig Isaac Norman Henkel Emmannuel Ambroise Diggs presently found himself. He might have been known as Oz the Great and Powerful, but the longer he spent chasing the elusive knowledge contained within the Wyrds' library, the more he began to see his skills as a researcher being equal to the less ignoble abbreviation of his latter names, Pinhead. For surely, he should have found *something* by now if there had ever been anything to find.

The Wizard put down the latest book he had been reading and pinched his fingers across the bridge of his nose. Even *he* was beginning to get a headache after reading a dozen different volumes debating the existence of reason. Yet what else was there to do? Without searching, he could never hope to find anything – assuming there was anything *to* find, of course – and yet, as vain as his search appeared to be, there was literally nothing else he had to go on. And therefore, continuing to search – even when his search looked more and more a waste of time –

was at the very least doing *something* as opposed to doing *nothing*.

Oscar's mind wandered back to the brief visit of the Cheshire Cat. Was that yesterday? The day before? It was so impossible to tell in a place that did not seem to have a nighttime. All time, in fact, seemed to run together, without there being any concept by which one could tell its passing. The old man had found himself waking from naps he had fallen into, so even a logical guess would have been difficult – too much time had been lost to sleep to accurately gauge the passage of time from observation alone.

The Wizard had encountered the Cat on three separate occasions now. Twice before reaching the Wyrds' Castle, and once since he had arrived. In the two previous encounters, the Cheshire's presence had seemed more like an effort to goad him in a specific direction – which had ultimately been the castle itself. But this last time – though he had indeed imparted some useful bits of information – his presence had yielded absolutely nothing in the way of guidance. It appeared for all intents and purposes that the Cheshire had just come to toy with him. Like any other cat might with a strand of yarn blowing in the wind...

Of course, when the Wizard had encountered the feline before, the Cat could not simply come out and say, "You need to go to the old castle over yonder, and this is how you get there." Oh no – the Wizard always had to figure out what the Cat was getting at on his own, and it had never actually been while the Cat was there. It was always later that the Wizard had figured out that where he had ended up was precisely where the Cheshire had wanted him to go all along.

With this in mind, Oscar had found his mind drifting time and again back to his last meeting with the Cheshire Cat, searching for some subtle clue or suggestion which might have been an effort of the Cat to impart something useful, some kind of signpost which would send the Wizard along the proper path, give him some kind of inclination as to where to search for the information on how to undo the magic which the Wyrds had cast and to bring them back to Wonderland. Yet no matter how many times he revisited the conversation in his mind, the Wizard could find no double-meaning, no subliminal suggestion intended to give the Wizard any kind of direction in his search.

Once more, Oscar found his mind wandering as memories of his time before his grandiose aspirations to rule the magical kingdom of Oz had ever polluted his mind. There was one point in time that all he ever thought of magic was as a way to trick and manipulate people. He was not even a slight of hand magician of any skill in the outside world. His only claims to talent had been his ventriloquism and his skill in managing a hot air balloon – though the latter was arguably not his strongest talent, as he would not have found Oz in the first place if he had been a better balloon pilot. In fact, those talents had been his advertised skills when he had gone to work for Bailum & Barney's Great Consolidated Show – being a ventriloquist who would go up in a hot air balloon to draw attention to the circus.

But this did not mean that Oscar did not have the opportunity to learn a trick or two from the resident magician of the circus, Mindred. Though he billed himself as a voyeur of the mind, in truth the man had been a slight of hand master who used his not-so-small skills of misdirection to convince people that he was able to move objects with his thoughts alone. In fact, that was Mindred's most invaluable lesson to Oscar:

Always distract the rubes from what you are actually doing. So long as you keep them looking to your left hand, they never think of what you are doing with your right.

When Oscar had found himself in Oz, it had been Mindred's philosophy which had given him the unique opportunity to convince the people of the magical land that he was an impossibly powerful wizard, and it had been upon the coattails of that deception that had let him rule unopposed over Oz for countless years.

The old man chuckled at the memory of his own words when he was found out by Dorothy. *I have been making believe.*

Oscar sat bolt upright. Was it that simple?

Before he realized it, the Wizard found himself pacing to and fro in the room, his mind abuzz with thoughts and ideas. Why had he not seen it sooner?

Now it was not his own words he thought of, but those of the Cat. The Cheshire had told him all along and the old man had been taking the Cat at his word – his *literal* word. But what if the Cat had only been making believe by using words that suggested one thing that was not *actually* what they were?

In as much as it is where I live, had said the Cat in reference to the Wyrds' Castle, *but not perhaps in the sense you wish it to be.* He had also said that he had lived in *all four* castles - *with the Wyrds!*

But that had not been the way of it. The Cat had said so himself. *I gave up my tasks to each, and then simply wandered as my feline whims guided me.*

The Cheshire Cat had not lived in any of the castles – he had wandered Wonderland. But he had said that he had, all the same. It had never been a statement of fact, at all.

It had been a riddle: How does one exist in five different places at the same time?

Suddenly, the Wizard stopped and looked around him. All at once, he knew the answer.

By leaving parts of yourself in different places. And only in a place like Wonderland – where things that would otherwise be impossible – could such a concept actually exist.

The Cheshire Cat had not been suggesting that *he* had lived with the Wyrds – but that *parts* of himself had. Or, to be more specific, the minutia of knowledge that had comprised the tasks he had given the poor lost girls whom he had turned into Wyrds. The trivial facts of existence – the Cat's concepts of reality from before the Wyrds had come to Wonderland – had been given to the Wyrds more than just symbolically. They had *literally* been given to the girls to use in the embodiment of their tasks – in the form of books. Volumes and volumes of books.

Which meant this had never been one of the Wyrd's own libraries, at all – it had been the Cat's. All of these otherwise worthless details had existed long before the Wyrds had come up with their plan to escape Wonderland. And – now that the Wizard gave it thought – it was why Mombi's book had been found outside one of the castle libraries. Because the Wyrds would never have put a book of their own creation into a library that was actually the mind of the Cheshire Cat made manifest!

"I'm right, aren't I?" asked Oscar aloud. "I have been digging through the recesses of *your* thoughts, haven't I?"

The Wizard was quiet for a moment, listening for any response. Somehow, instinctively, he knew the Cheshire Cat could hear his every word. And that if he waited, sooner or later, the Cat would speak up.

But it was not the Cat the Wizard heard as he strained through the silence – it was the sound of a trumpet. A blaring trumpet like one would hear announcing the arrival of royalty – or a call to arms. It was still distant, but it was growing nearer with every blast of noise it made.

The old man dashed to the window to look out down upon the grounds surrounding the castle. "Of all the..."

Oscar wasted no time in rushing out of the library and down the stairs. In moments he was at the door to the castle and he flung it open, yet refusing to take a step outside into the chaos which had erupted all around him.

All about him, creatures were running to and fro, some of them shaped like over-sized playing cards, and others appearing to be animals re-imagined as people. As he stood safely within the doorway, a large hare dressed in some kind of ball gown rushed past the door, the hem of his dress hiked high to either side of his body to keep from tripping over it.

In a moment, the oddly dressed creature had disappeared along the side of the castle, to be replaced instead by two of the card people entwined in each other's grasp upon the ground. With each of the cards' hands which emerged from its sides locked in the other, the cards had managed to each bend themselves into half circles, together forming an oblong shape that gave them the capacity to roll along the ground like some kind of ill-conceived wheel.

From somewhere in the distance, the Wizard could hear a feminine voice raised above the clamor shouting, "Off with his head! Bring me his head! Off with it, off with it *NOW!*"

The Wizard had no difficulty identifying the speaker, either. The Queen of Hearts had come calling upon his doorstep. This had been then woman who had called for his own head when he had stepped forward to defend the King of Hearts from his own beheading. Oscar had not been the least concerned for his own safety – he had simply grown tall with his magic word and walked away. But Dorothy had forewarned him that his intervention had led to some kind of Wonderland civil war, and it was clear that the conflict had finally reached as far as the Wyrds' Castle itself.

Once again, the blaring trumpet was heard over the melee, and the Wizard caught sight for the first time of its cause – a large white rabbit came bursting into the meadow from the trees, blasting a horn with all his might. Oscar also recognized this creature after a moment – Dorothy had called him simply the White Rabbit, and when last he had been here, he had accompanied the King of Hearts. But he had ended up running away, with the King fast upon his heels for betraying the crown.

The rabbit lowered the horn and shouted something, though the ruckus prevented his words from reaching the Wizard's ears initially. But the creature was running full tilt in the old man's direction, and within the space of a minute, the White Rabbit's words became clear.

"The King is here," called the rabbit. "All hail the King!"

"I was already here, Rabbit," came a voice from amidst the clamor. No sooner did the voice sound, than possibly the oddest dressed man the Wizard had ever seen bounded over the body of what appeared to be an otter and landed with amazing agility in the path of the rabbit. With one hand, the man maintained his balance, while with the other, he held tightly to a crown he wore upon his head. "Though it would seem that we are not actually alone, and it might not be so clever to tell the Queen where I am. She seems a might upset by something."

"Not you," gasped the rabbit, dodging around the man while jabbing a finger behind himself. "Him!"

Immediately, another man came racing out of the crowd, following the rabbit into the midst of the conflict, waving a large lance back and forth to clear his way. "Get back here, traitor!" called the man whom the Wizard immediately recognized as the King of Hearts. The newly arrived King seemed completely oblivious to the war being raged around him in his blind pursuit of the White Rabbit. "I am not through smiting at you!"

The rabbit ducked behind the strangely dressed man, grabbing the man's shoulders to keep him positioned between himself and the King of Hearts. "Your Majesty, it is a revolution!" called the creature. "I brought you to the war so that you could see I was not a traitor!"

The strangely dressed man with the crown upon his head twisted his head back at as far an angle as he could, obviously trying – and failing – to let his eyes look upon the rabbit who clung to his backside. The effect however sent the two dancing in a circle as the man chased the White Rabbit in a constantly revolving effort to see the creature holding onto him. "I say, I don't think you're supposed to grab hold of the King, Rabbit. I am almost certain of that."

The King of Hearts stopped in his tracks at the strange man's words. "King? You, Hatter? Have you gone mad?"

The man whom the King of Hearts had called Hatter came to an abrupt halt in his chase of the rabbit, sending the creature flying off and into a sprawl upon the ground. The White Rabbit dodged a foot from one of the other combatants and in the hair of a breath was once again on his feet, running for the castle door.

"Help me!" cried the rabbit, spying the Wizard standing there. Before the Wizard could respond, the rabbit had reached him and clasped ahold of the lapels of his coat, his eyes large and wide with fear. "I'm fighting in the revolution! And you have the only castle to seize!"

Oscar was beside himself with confusion. The White Rabbit was talking of revolution, the King of Hearts was now scuffling with some Hatter-usurper for possession of the crown which the odd man had been wearing, and the Queen of Hearts was somewhere out there shouting for *someone's* head. How could he *possibly* be of any help to anyone with this much chaos all around?

"What would you have me do?" asked the Wizard, thrusting the rabbit's hands away.

"Sanctuary!" cried the White Rabbit, beating at his own strange vest. "My armor has clean fallen away, and I have nothing to keep myself from harm!"

"You should have thought of that before you decided to work for more than one side," pronounced the Wizard, hoping that his manner projected wisdom and calm. In truth, he was just as panicked by the battle all around him as the rabbit was.

"But I've won," insisted the rabbit. "The revolution is here, and only your castle will stand when it's done! Soon, the crown will fall – all three of them – and you will be the only one left to rule. For a King needs a castle, and I have come to serve the new King!"

"Oh no," objected the Wizard, waving his hands emphatically in front of him. "I have made the mistake of trying to be king of all I see, and it ended badly. Very, very badly. And I won't have anymore of that!"

"Then," said the White Rabbit, darting a furtive glance in both directions before he continued, "can I take over then? I'd be ever so good at it. Just ask the King and Queen of Hearts – I have been the most loyal member of their court forever!"

Oscar closed his eyes and shook his head. Only here in Wonderland could one reason that a life of service somehow qualified one for being a king – and this coming from the single most *disloyal* member that he could imagine.

Suddenly, above the tumult of the battle, a new voice could be heard. "To me, my army," yelled the new voice, "To me and away from this battle if you wish to live to fight another day!"

The Wizard looked past the White Rabbit and saw the large brown hare whom had he had seen wearing a dress before – though now the creature had divested of the garment – waving his arms high over his head to get attention. And in one of his hands he now held the crown which the two would-be kings had been wrestling for.

Without waiting a moment longer, the large brown rabbit took off running, and to the Wizard's amazement, the warring factions stopped their fighting and took off in the direction the hare now led. In moments, the meadow before the castle was clear save for the two dusty grapplers and a collapsed litter to the far side of the field, shattered by what appeared to be a sudden drop to the ground. And from amidst the rubble of the conveyance rose a scarlet-dressed woman whose face was as fiercely crimson as her garb.

"Off with their heads!" shouted the Queen of Hearts. "Off with *all* of their heads!"

The Hatter rose out of the dirt, brushing himself off. The King of Hearts remained seated upon the ground, his arms resting crossed upon his knees. Looking after where the hare had marched off with the royal army, the King let out a heavy sigh, then lowered his head to rest upon his arms.

"I must say," said the Hatter, "I just cannot believe that the Hare would take my army like that. It was completely unexpected."

The Queen of Hearts came storming across the former field of battle, aiming for the Hatter. "Off with your head!" she screamed.

The Hatter looked to either side of himself and raised his arms to helplessly. "There does not appear to be anyone about to take it, I'm afraid."

The Queen came to a halt, visibly confused. "Take it yourself!" she bellowed after a moment.

"Then who should present it to you?" asked the Hatter innocently.

"You must take it *and* give it to me!"

The Hatter scratched at his head. "I suppose I could try," he reasoned, "though I fear if I do not succeed, you will only have my head again for it."

"Enough!" yelled the Wizard. He pushed aside the White Rabbit – who reverently bowed as he stepped aside – and stormed up to the feuding duo. "This war is over!"

The Queen and Hatter looked blankly at the Wizard, while the King of Hearts looked up blinking. "Then who won?" asked the King.

Oscar thought fast. "The White Rabbit," at this the Wizard pointed behind him at the creature he could imagine cowering in his wake. "He caused the war, and so if it is over, he must be the winner."

The Hatter hunched his shoulders and gave a conspiratorial look to the royals on either side of him. "Does this mean we get to court martial him?"

"No, of course not," said the Wizard. "You'll be lucky if he doesn't court martial you!"

At this, all three of the would-be royals flinched visibly.

"Now, off with you all! I don't have time for this nonsense!" The Wizard made a shooing motion with his hands, then made to walk back into the castle.

"But where do we go?" asked the King, rising up from his seated position.

"Oh, for all the love of..." *Like lecturing to five year olds!* groaned Oscar inwardly.

The old man turned around and took on the most commanding wizardly presence he could manage. "You two," to which he jabbed his finger at first the King and then Queen, "need to go back to your own castle and act like a proper King and Queen. And no more of this, 'Off with his or her head' nonsense!

"As for you," said the Wizard, directing his finger at the Hatter, "I don't care *where* you go, just find some place other than here to be!" Oscar made to make a commanding departure by turning on his heel, only to find himself face-to-whisker with the White Rabbit. The Rabbit's nose twitched nervously. "And you, too. Find someplace else to be!"

Stepping around the Rabbit, the Wizard Oz walked across the threshold of the Wyrds' Castle and slammed the door behind him, not waiting to see if any of the four actually did what he had said.

Always leave them wanting more, thought Oz the Great and Powerful to himself. *And in this case, I could not possibly have given them more if I had wanted to!*

Chapter 10

Toto To the Rescue

If there was one thing you never intruded upon, it was an animal's personal territory. Regardless of whether that animal were a large Hungry Tiger from Quadling Country or a tiny black dog from Kansas, one simply did not rush blindly into their territory uninvited without consequences.

This was what Toto insisted on telling himself as he marched down the corridors of the Emerald Palace. He might be small, but he was still a fearsome beast, and no Wicked Witch was going to come into his territory without facing his wrath. However, unlike the Hungry Tiger, Toto considered himself a fairly intelligent beast – to which he owed his association with Dorothy and her friends for. This was not to say that the Tiger was *not* intelligent, only that the great cat was truly no different than any other of his species, in spite of his size: he would rather pounce first before taking the time to consider the field of battle.

Of course, Toto chose to ignore that this was precisely what he had intended to do before the Cheshire Cat had stopped him. But again, one did not give credit to a cat anymore than one needed – it was undignified.

Regardless of the situation though, Toto did have a direction and a purpose. He was on a straight course for the Emerald Throne Room. He knew that the Witch posing as Ozma was in the Princess' chambers, so she would not be there. But there would be someone in the Throne Room.

Over the last several days, there had been a stranger constantly at Ozma's side – a young Munchkin lad. Toto had not cared for him and so had not previously engaged the man in conversation. Especially since, as a general rule, Toto rather disliked speaking at all, which only lent to the aversion to doing so with the newcomer. Initially, the dog had trusted the Princess, and so had thought nothing of her new companion. Yet now in light of learning that the Princess was *not* the Princess, after all – well, the young man took on an entirely unappealing aspect which the canine intended to address before he decided to directly confront the fake Ozma.

That this Munchkin was the only one of the new arrivals to not actually have magic at his disposal had no effect upon the dog's decision, of course. Well – very little. Toto needed information, and there was no one else left in the castle to ask. And he certainly was not going to dignify the thought of trying to search about the castle to find out where the Cheshire had run off to.

Not when there was a much easier target to find, who would likely know a great deal more than any feline would.

Toto reached the Throne Room and paused, sniffing at the air. Though he could detect a lingering scent from Mombi, the peculiar odor belonging to her spoiled magic was not present here – but the smell belonging to the Munchkin lad was. Which meant – if the Cheshire's opinion could be given any credibility – that the young man was not someone or something else changed into a Munchkin. He was apparently precisely what he appeared to be.

The dog quickly looked about the room and soon found the object of his search – the young man was sitting on the lowest-most step of the throne's dais. Wasting not a moment more, the little dog raced across the room, a growl building deep within his chest as he ran.

The Munchkin spotted Toto when he was only halfway across the room. But Toto had not been trying to be stealthy like some cat, so it did not slow him in the least. He was a dog, after all, and dogs did not lurk – they charged.

"Why, hello there," said the young man, perking up at the site of the little dog racing over to him. "The Queen has been looking for you." The man seemed oblivious to Toto's threat as he stood up casually as if to welcome an old friend into the room.

Toto did not slow down as the young man reached out a hand in greeting. The little black dog instead leaped into the air and bit down into the stranger's hand, eliciting a loud cry from his prey.

"Hey!" cried the Munchkin, pulling his hand protectively to his chest. "What'd you do that for? I was only going to pet you! I was told you were nice!"

Toto let out a gruff bark, and let the growl in his throat rise in volume. He raced in and nipped at the man's ankle, causing his victim to step away and stumble backwards onto the stairs. The small canine did not relent, continuing to nip at the man's legs, forcing him to crawl backwards up the stairs to get away from his attacker.

"Stop already," cried the young man. "Why are you biting me?"

Toto stopped his thrusting and stood stolidly at the base of the stairs. "You work for a Wicked Witch," accused Toto. *Oh, how I hate to have to talk – but if I don't, this will get me nothing.* With that thought, Toto made to lunge forward and watched in amusement as the man pulled his leg quickly up and out of range of the dog's teeth.

"No, no," insisted the young man, who quickly scurried behind Ozma's throne for protection. "I brought her message, sure, but I don't work for her."

"I know about Ozma!" barked Toto. "I know that's not Ozma who you've been helping. That's a Wicked Witch. That's Mombi!"

Of course, the latter was mostly an educated guess, since he only had the Cheshire's deductions to back up his puzzling out the impostor's identity. But from how wide the young man's eyes grew and the level of fear that suddenly filled the air, Toto's guess was instantly confirmed.

"Okay, okay," yelled the young man. "I confess! It's Mombi! But what was I supposed to do? I couldn't *not* help her! She's a witch!"

Toto growled louder and raced up the stairs, barking twice sharply as he ran. When he reached the top of the steps, he stopped abruptly. The young Munchkin clung ever tighter to the back of the Emerald Throne, his eyes clenched shut. Tears rolled down his cheeks and his voice had taken on a blubbering nature, as well.

"Please, please, please," sobbed the young man. "I was only doing it to save Miradel! I wouldn't have done it if she didn't have Miradel!"

Toto allowed the growl in his throat to lesson. "Who's Miradel?"

The young man panted fervently for several seconds without a response, forcing the dog to ask again. "Who is Miradel?"

At last, the young man must have realized that Toto was *not* going to bite him again and he opened his eyes. "My sweetheart," he said. The depth of sadness and hopelessness in his voice convinced the little dog in an instant that the young man's words were true. "They took her. The witches did."

Toto's own eyes grew wide. "Witches? Witch-*es*? As in more than one?"

The young man nodded his head feverishly. "Two of them. Mombi and another one. I never knew her name. I know she looked a lot like the Wicked Witch of the East – the one Dorothy Gale dropped her house on. But Mombi said things to the other witch, things to remind her how to act if people were to believe she really was the Wicked Witch, so I'm pretty sure that it was only a disguise.

"They both took Miradel into the old witch's castle in Munchkin Land, and I never saw her after that. When Mombi came back out, she said I would have to take a message to Ozma in the Emerald City if I ever wanted to see my dear, sweet Miradel ever again. She says," the young man pitched his voice high to imitate the witch and continued, "'Bartus, my dear boy, you do this one thing for me, and you can have your sweet back in but a couple of days.' So I agreed to do it, because it was the only way I could get Miradel back."

Toto sat on his haunches, going over what the Munchkin was relating. "Go on."

"Well, Mombi came along with me, but she changed herself into a cricket so no one else would see her. She mostly hid in my pocket, but lots of times she would come up to my shoulder where she could tell me things. And make sure I had her message right."

The Munchkin released his grip upon the back of the throne tentatively as he continued to talk. "When we got here, I gave the message, just like she said."

"What was the message?"

"That Ozma was supposed to let me bring the 'girl who is not of Oz' east to Munchkin Land, where the other witch could confront her. But Ozma insisted that I should not escort her, but that the Good Witch Glinda would instead. I thought Mombi would be really upset by this, but she only laughed once we were alone again, and ran off to who-knows-where."

The Munchkin collapsed upon his posterior with a sigh. "Well, I suppose I do know where, because after that when I next saw Ozma, she told me she wasn't the Princess anymore. She told me she was Mombi, and that I had to keep working for her in the Emerald Palace. I just wanted to go back to get Miradel, but Mombi wouldn't let me."

"What about all the servants? What did you do to them?"

"I didn't do anything," insisted the young man. "I supposed that Mombi was getting rid of them the same way she did the Princess."

"And what did she do with Ozma? The real Ozma?" demanded the dog, his hackles rising at the thought of harm coming to the Princess.

"I can only guess," said the young man who had called himself Bartus, throwing his hands up. "She changes things. She turns them into other things. Saw her do that lots of times. I would guess she changed the Princess and all the rest of the people into other things. But I have no idea what. She doesn't tell me anything."

"So why do you stand guard here for her?"

"I don't. She just... smells bad. You notice it if you stay around her for a long while. Well, she didn't used to. Only after she became Ozma did that happen. Or it might have been when she started playing with that golden belt. Hard to say."

The magic belt! Toto had forgotten all about the vastly powerful artifact which Dorothy had given to Ozma. If the witch could master its power, Mombi would be unstoppable!

"But it got so's I couldn't stand it," continued the young man, "so I started staying here rather than with her in her room. And she didn't mind being left alone, either, so it worked."

Toto nodded his head once. All of that made perfect sense. "Well, I'm sorry for biting you then," he announced. "I thought you were one of her helpers. See, I'm going to go deal with her, and I needed to know if you were going to help her or not." Not an entirely true statement, but not entirely untrue either, the canine assured himself. He had not known what he would do after he confronted the witch's henchman, but now with the Magic Belt involved, there was a new urgency to exposing Mombi's deception.

Bartus' eyes grew wide again. "Oh, you shouldn't do that. She'll just turn *you* into something, then I really would be all alone in here."

"So come with me," offered Toto. "Help me deal with the Wicked Witch and we can help get your girl back."

"I can't," objected the young man. "I'd just end up getting her mad, and I wouldn't be doing anything for Miradel. No, no. Sorry, little dog. I can't help you."

Toto thought about this for a moment, then shrugged and turned away. "Suit yourself," he grunted. "I don't have time for a coward, anyhow."

Definitely would not have made a good dog, thought Toto as he raced out of the Throne Room. He knew as much as he was going to know now, and he could think of no further reason to put off what needed doing. But he did have a *very* good reason for doing it now – if Bartus were coward enough to be afraid to fight Mombi, he would just as likely have no compunction against telling the Wicked Witch of the little dog's plan if he thought it would somehow get him back to his precious Miradel.

Well, I just hope if he does get his girl back, that she won't ever learn how much of a craven her man was through all of this. No faster way to lose a girl than that, and it'd be a shame to lose her after all he's not *done to get her back.*

Toto shrugged aside thoughts of the young Munchkin as he raced through the hallways towards Princess Ozma's chambers. He knew enough now that the thing he needed to avoid was letting Mombi get the chance to cast her magic on him. Which meant, like any other of the countless times he had avoided being ensorceled, he needed to keep moving. Normally, he would have others who would help keep attention completely focused off of him as he darted about, so this time he would have to be especially fast – fast enough to count for two dogs, not just his one diminutive self.

As the dog raced up the hall to the Princess' room, one regret did cross his mind – it was too bad that he could not have convinced young Bartus to come along. One of the greatest banes of his existence was a closed door, and if Ozma's chamber door was shut, his rush to battle would be stunted.

Nothing worse than a battle charge needing to wait for the door to open.

As fate would have it, however, as Toto raced along the hall to his destination, he could see Ozma herself stepping out of her door. The thought briefly crossed his mind that he could battle the witch in the hall, but memory of the Magic Belt made him reconsider. He needed to know if the witch wore it or not, and with all the robes the faker wore, she could easily have it hidden beneath. No, he needed to find if the belt was where it belonged in the room, and to do that, he needed to get past Mombi.

Toto barked loudly, hoping to distract the witch-in-disguise long enough to keep the door open. The newly-named Queen of Oz hesitated, looking up – and that was all the little dog needed. With a renewed burst of energy, Toto darted past the would-be-Ozma and into the Princess' room.

"Why you little--" yelled Ozma's voice. "Get back here!" The fake Princess turned about and followed the dog back into her room.

Toto raced under the bed, trying to keep himself out of the witch's direct line of sight while he scanned the room. Normally, there was a drawer in the bureau where Ozma kept the belt when she was not using it, but much like the problem with the door, the canine could not be expected to open that on his own. Except, as he looked from his hiding spot at the drawer, he discovered it open. Whether the belt remained inside, he could not say – but Mombi had clearly been tampering with it.

"Get out here, you mongrel!" called Ozma's voice. "Get out from under my bed! You don't belong in here!"

Toto barked loudly, then rushed to the opposite side of the bed from where he had been hiding. Just as he reached the far side, he looked back and saw Ozma's face glare at him from where he had just been, just as he had planned.

In an instant, the small black dog had darted out from under the bed, did a quick turn and leaped up onto the bed itself. His hope had been to get a better vantage to see inside the drawer, but his eye was caught by something else – the Magic Picture was moving!

Normally, the Picture was a window through which any place in the world could be seen – as if the person commanding the Picture truly were just looking through a pane of glass. Yet when last Toto had been in the room, the Magic Picture had frozen upon an image of Dorothy standing on a great lawn in Oxford, England, directly alongside a stone wall. That was where he and his friend had been sent by the Magic Belt when Ozma had sent them after the Wizard. But when Ozma had used the Belt to again return them to Oz, only Toto had come back – with the new girl he and Dorothy had met in Oxford, Alice Liddell. Ever since then, the Magic Picture had been uncharacteristically frozen, showing only Dorothy standing still in the frame.

Now, the Picture was once again moving, showing a new place – what appeared to be a cultivated flower garden with a shadowy silhouette moving about the walkways between the flower beds. And after a moment, Toto's heart leaped when he saw who it was: Dorothy was once again visible within the glass – and though she was running, she was clearly safe and sound!

So distracted was Toto by the new image in the glass, he nearly forgot what he was about. Had he allowed himself to forget for a fraction of a second longer, he would have been undone, for at that moment, the fake Ozma moved to pounce upon her canine intruder. Toto dodged out of the way, with the self-proclaimed Queen calling out an "ah-ha!" a fraction too soon.

The dog bounded back to the floor and raced back to the far side of the bed, barking again. He bounded into the air for emphasis, goading the disguised witch into a rage. But as he felt himself falling back to the floor, the hairs between his ears singed as energy shot past him. Had he been in the air a moment longer, he would have been struck full-on with the witch's magic.

Back under the bed the canine ran, green sparks following him as he ran. This time, he did not wait to see if the witch were following, but darted ninety degrees and ran out the bottom side of the bed at full tilt. He took a running leap at the drawer where the belt was. Unfortunately, even with his momentum, he could only barely get his legs around the lip of the drawer – and with no actual hands, his purchase on the drawer was short lived, his paws scratching and scrabbling helplessly.

But before he lost his grip, he saw what he was after – the Magic Belt was still in the drawer, its golden, jewel-encrusted surface reflecting the green light of a newly fired blast of energy as it fell away from his vision.

"So that's what you're after," laughed fake-Ozma, in an oddly cackling voice. "It's worthless, you stupid dog! It can only grant one wish a day, and I have already tried it out today!"

Toto cursed himself, for he did remember Dorothy talking about that once upon a time – how the Belt could only be used once each day. And if what Mombi said was true, even if he could reach the Belt, he could not use it in any way to help himself. But he had also known Ozma to use the Belt several times in the same day. So there was a chance...

The canine gave the briefest thought to running away, but a quick glance at the door showed that was no longer an option. The witch had closed the door after her. So as soon as his feet hit the floor, he was once again bounding for the underside of the bed.

Out of the corner of his eye, Toto could see the witch's arm following him, and he dodged away from the safety of the bed just in time to see the green energy burst in front of him, changing the bed covers into a pile of sand.

A quick examination of the room gave the dog a new direction, as he headed for the chair situated between the bed and bureau. The chair's cushion would provide him a spring that the floor lacked, and he imagined that he could use it to once more launch himself at the Magic Belt. Working or not, he felt he had to at the very least try for it. He truly had no other options.

However, when he pounced into the chair, the small dog almost lost his footing entirely when he found himself landing atop an over-sized green emerald. The smell of the thing offended his nose...

Emerald's don't smell. The thought flashed across Toto's mind and a chill ran along his spine. *Emeralds* did not smell, but magically disguised *Princesses* might. In shock, the small dog froze, realizing that he had actually found the real Ozma – the witch had transformed her into an emerald!

Too late, Toto realized his mistake as a hand crushed down upon the scruff of his neck. "Ha!" cried the fake-Ozma in victory. All Toto could do was look down helplessly at the glowing facets of the gemstone, powerless to do anything with his discovery. He had been so close to saving the Princess, but now...

A loud crash echoed from across the room. "Stop!" a sharp voice barked. "Put him down, or I'll... I'll make you regret it!"

Toto was stunned to see the Munchkin lad, Bartus, standing in the doorway. He had no weapon, no defense. He had just burst into the room – and given Toto the distraction he needed!

Twisting about, Toto sunk his teeth into the disguised witch's arm. With a cry of pain, the fake-Ozma released her grip, and the dog pushed off with his hind feet, sending himself flailing into the air.

His aim proved true, however, and the small canine found himself landing upon the bureau. He missed the drawer, but only by a short distance. It took him a bare moment of scrambling to get his feet beneath him and he bounded into the drawer. He laid himself as flat as he could against the Magic Belt, and closed his eyes.

"Bring Dorothy--"

The small dog never finished his wish. The world around him exploded in light and he instead found himself falling...

Chapter 11

A Return To Oz

Dorothy could not recall anyone ever describing how they had trouble leaving a place. Finding one, certainly – there were all kinds of stories of people who searched for a place, and even more about going on long, elaborate quests to find one. But there were no stories of how finding ones way away from a place had ever been all that terribly challenging.

Yet this was precisely the circumstance the girl from Kansas found herself in. She had rushed out of the study where the exit from the Looking Glass World had been with the expectation that the garden would be immediately outside. That had plainly been a wholly misplaced idea. For beyond the study, there was simply a hallway with more books stacked to the ceiling. Though there were windows now at a level through which the girl could see the outside, none of these showed anything more than several brownish and red buildings built, presumably, from large bricks. And even those were fading from view with the failing light of day.

In fact, it was definitely more dark than light outside now. The Kansas girl could even see stars blinking into existence in the sky.

As to the interior, Dorothy found it fascinating how the bookshelves were actually built into the walls in most places, giving the illusion that the books were part of the building itself. This was clearly a very old building, with the walls being made entirely of a dark wood polished with a lacquer that suggested the wood had been polished again and again for centuries. At least, it all appeared quite old, with even pillars in places along the wall being constructed of the dark wood.

Dorothy quickly found a spiral staircase leading down, yet the first floor of the building was no better than the upper – all that changed was that more of the walls seemed composed of solid white stone than the wooden ones on the upper floor. There were still more books lining the walls, and though this level seemed comprised more of segmented rooms than a giant hall like the upper level, it was still plain that this was a very old building.

Overall, the building was not quite a castle, but it did not give the appearance entirely of being a library, either. There did not seem to be the organization that the girl had found common in the repositories she had visited. It was clear that the residents of this building coveted books, but the appearance was more of a beloved selection – albeit a large one – than an archive of any kind.

The eerie silence of the building gave Dorothy goosebumps. Alice had described this place as a school, a university. She claimed it was the largest in all of England. Or had that been just in Oxford? Knowing that this was a school, Dorothy could imagine that the place would be empty towards evening, with the students and teachers returning to their own homes and residences. Yet the effect of walking these halls uninterrupted was still an unnerving feeling.

After a bit more searching, the girl found the exit and slowly opened the right-most wooden double door to look outside. She took comfort in finding that at least the building was not locked. Which meant if she were discovered, there would be less concern about whether she had broken in.

Seeing no one about, Dorothy stepped out into a paved courtyard outside. Though a courtyard might have been a bit of an overstatement – the stone-paved area was somewhat wider where the door opened, but it quickly tapered to a narrower walkway between another building and a stone wall. Apparently in this school, even outside was much like walking the halls inside – only there was no roof. At least not in all the areas, since there were some areas that descended into covered archways.

Now this *looks more like a castle*, thought the girl.

Being outside, Dorothy was convinced that she still only needed to find her way beyond the cluster of buildings and into the garden. Her search for some kind of sign which might have pointed her in the right direction proved fruitless, and therefore she was forced to walk along the pathways in hopes of finding it on her own.

The Kansas girl's sense of direction was completely gone, of course. No internal compass existed when you were thrown between four different realms of reality in as many days. This might have been the world of her birth, but at night, there was just no way she could tell where any specific direction lay, much less in which direction she should go.

More than once her heart had leaped when she caught sight of what appeared to be a patch of greenery in the dark, but it was never the familiar great lawn where she had originally appeared in Oxford. Twice, she had entered courtyards with grass growing within the walls of the estate. The first had been an area where the grass was maintained in five patches over gravel, the overall pattern suggesting a flower and its petals. The second had resembled a large circle with an "X" cut away and overlaid with gravel. At the center of this second area had been a large fountain.

Everywhere she went, Dorothy saw signs of the season – leaves turning brown and the grass having that all-too-familiar look of autumn to it. In Oz, there really were no lawns of grass, except what the Wizard had grown for himself in the Emerald City, but Dorothy could well remember how things looked in Kansas as she was growing up. Judging by all around her, it was either late autumn or perhaps early winter if the snow were late in coming. It had been full-on winter in the Looking Glass World, but that was hardly a guide by which to follow in the real world. For all she knew, it could have been winter there all year round.

In many places, the girl could see trees stretching over the high walls, and several times she attempted to climb up the walls to see what lay on the other side. At best, in a few places she could manage to pull herself up to the edge of the walls, but she never could tell what lay beyond in the darkened areas beyond. And rather than risk landing in an area she could not return from, she elected to stay on the paved paths of the school.

Besides, had thought Dorothy, *wherever I must go must've been someplace Alice could've gone, and I can't imagine her climbing walls to get there.*

Still, none of the areas she did find resembled the high walls with the field stretching out towards the trees in the distance that she was looking for. And until Dorothy discovered this specific area, she could never find the Rabbit Hole leading back to Wonderland.

As she wandered, Dorothy did see a few people mingling in the distance, but she always kept her distance. No matter how much the comfort of knowing that the buildings not being locked was a sign that she could not be charged with some kind of burglary, she would still be hard-pressed to explain who she was and why she was wearing what to most anyone would appear to be a brilliant green formal dress. And if she were escorted out of the school, how could she ever find the gardens?

At least if she were discovered, Dorothy took heart in knowing her dress would not make her appear a vagabond. Say whatever one liked about the style of her wardrobe, the material with which her dresses were made in Oz were undeniably sturdy. After stumbling down a rabbit hole, running through woods, and even fighting her way through snow, the outfit had not torn nor frayed in any way. Even after all her adventures over the last few days, her clothes looked clean and well-tended, something any fabric from outside of Oz could never have boasted.

Hours seemed to pass as Dorothy searched through the stone corridors. But in the dark, she had difficulty determining whether one path was any different from another. She was certain that she must have crossed and re-crossed her own path several times already. Yet she had no way to look for any kind of landmark, so she could not be entirely certain. She passed several other buildings as she went, but she elected to not explore any of them – there was no answer in going inside, she assured herself.

The satchel had proven awkward and cumbersome when carried for this long, as well. More than once, Dorothy had stopped to either lay down her burden or to refasten the material holding the broken mirror and book inside. All of this would have been for naught if she did not at least carry away her prizes. She considered briefly the idea of hiding the satchel and returning after she found the garden, but common sense led her to casting that idea aside. She was lost enough without trying to find her way back to some hiding spot in the dark. And there was certainly no guarantee she could navigate back to the spot and then once again to the garden.

Whether by chance or design, eventually Dorothy came upon a walkway through a large wall and into what was clearly a well tended yard which most likely would have been flowery bushes lining the walls, if it were any other season. The grounds were kept up well enough that there were not a great deal of leavings under the bushes – at least not that she could see in the dark. But the bushes looked right all the same.

With this in mind, Dorothy decided to stop looking for flower gardens as she pictured them in her mind and instead look for areas where flowering plants grew. *Perhaps*, thought the girl, *a garden has not the same meaning to someone in England. Maybe it just means where green things grow.*

With this in mind, Dorothy quickly discovered that the more she explored this region of the university grounds, the more such areas she discovered. There were some limited areas where she found herself passing through walkways that did have old, dried flower patches growing along the walkway, but definitely not the wide-blooming fields of flowers she would have expected. But flowers were flowers, and that really was all she needed to find, if Alice's words were any indication.

A garden is for flowers. A wood is for tall trees, had said Alice. *Why would we have trees like that in a garden?*

Dorothy felt a renewed sense of confidence as she reexamined Alice's words. The areas she was moving through now had plenty of bushes, but few trees. And though many of the trees were tall, they did not usually hang over anywhere that the flowers would have been growing.

And all at once, Dorothy walked through a passage through one of the walls and saw a wide open field with the shadows of a treeline in the distance. Looking back, she could with near certainty guess that this was where Alice was standing when the Kansas girl had first appeared. Exhilarated, Dorothy hitched her satchel more solidly across her shoulder and took off running for the trees...

...and just as suddenly found herself running towards a large, four posted bed! Dorothy could not stop herself as her legs hit the side and she went tumbling over the surface of the bed, her momentum rolling her over its surface and off the far side.

The fall from the bed had gouged the book into the Kansas girl's ribs once again, knocking the breath from her lungs. *I really should do something about that*, the girl thought as she held her side in pain. Stars flashed before her eyes, and she lay still trying to gather her wits about her. She could hear voices raised in the room – some kind of argument, though the meaning of the words being bantered around escaped her focus.

Finally, Dorothy rolled onto her back and pulled herself up over the edge of the green velvet covering to look across the room. There, she was met with a shock. A strange man was standing in the doorway, his hands raised in front of him, yelling at a girl with tight, bouncy yellow curls. The girl was holding something black in her outstretched arm – some kind of bag, perhaps.

Dorothy blinked hard to try to keep her head from spinning, then opened her eyes wide to see past the tears. In that instant, she recognized the girl as Ozma, and the object in her hand was – Toto! Ozma was shaking Toto roughly, and her faithful canine companion flew about limply as she did.

"Ozma!" cried Dorothy without thinking, standing and rushing to take the small black dog into her arms. "You're going to hurt Toto!"

Ozma turned on the Kansas girl with a face filled with rage, changing into shock and confusion at the sight of Dorothy. The small amount of resistance to the Kansas girl taking the dog melted away as the confusion took hold. "Where did you come from?!" demanded the Princess.

"I don't know," answered Dorothy, cradling Toto in her arms. "I was in England, heading for the Rabbit Hole and all of a sudden, I was here instead. Didn't you--"

The girl's words were cut short when she saw the strange man rush at the Princess from behind. "Ozma, look out!"

The Princess of Oz turned, but not quickly enough. The young man tackled her to the floor. In moments, the two were entangled in a wrestling match, with the stranger trying to grab at the Princess' arms to hold her down. Ozma, however, was much stronger than she appeared and looked to be winning the battle.

"Let Ozma go," commanded Dorothy, kicking at the young man as best she could without dropping poor Toto.

"Not.. Ozma..." gasped the young man, just as the Princess threw him off of her.

Ozma rose into a crouch and quickly surveyed the room. Her eyes darted from first Dorothy, and then to the young man. "He's... he's a spy, come to kill me, Dorothy," Ozma blurted out.

The stranger had managed to right himself by now, but instead of renewing his attack, he scrambled backwards to the wall and cowered there.

None of this made any sense to Dorothy. This stranger attacking Ozma, then retreating when his attack failed? Ozma was only a girl – what was this man so keenly afraid of that he had not been a moment before?

"She's the witch," said the young man, as if in answer to Dorothy's unspoken question. "Mombi. That's Mombi!"

"Why, that's just absurd," responded Dorothy, moving to stand in front of Ozma defensively. "This is Ozma, Princess of Oz. I know Mombi, and she does not look anything *like* Ozma."

"She changed herself," retorted the young man. Jerking his head sideways, he cried a warning. "Look out!"

If there was one thing years upon years of adventures had taught Dorothy, it was that when someone said to move like that, you moved. You did not ask questions and you did not stop to think why. You just moved. And it was the one instinct that saved her that day, as it had so many times before.

Just as Dorothy stepped to the side, a blast of green energy flashed by her, striking the wall directly above the man's head. Instantly, the wall transformed into a gooey substance that oozed down and into the young man's hair. He panicked and jumped up, trying to get the slimy substance out of his hair, while Dorothy turned to the only other person in the room.

Ozma was now standing, her hands held in a crooked posture at her waist. Yet what was more telling was that her hands were glowing – green.

A scowl ripped across the young Princess's beautiful face. "You will not be stopping me, Dorothy Gale of Kansas. I thought you gone, but if you are returned, you can share the same fate as your precious Ozma, as well!"

Another bolt of energy shot across the room as Ozma thrust her arm forward. Dorothy managed to duck, but only barely. Yet once down, she lost her balance and found herself upon her backside, unable to dodge any further.

Whether it was just a fortuitous moment or the sudden drop had shaken him awake, Toto came alive in that moment and leaped into the air at Ozma. The small dog's teeth sunk into the royal girl's hand, eliciting a shriek of pain. Ozma threw her arm wide and sent Toto sailing through the air, but the blood the small canine had drawn was plainly visible where he had bitten her.

Quickly, the Princess grabbed at her wounded hand, took another look about the room, then turned and fled through the open door, howling as she ran away. To Dorothy's ears, it sounded more like Ozma were crying than screaming though.

Dorothy considered giving chase, but instead got to her feet and went to check on her hero. "Toto, are you okay?"

The small black dog darted around the side of the bed, but did not pause to answer the girl's question. In an instant, the dog had run out the door after the Princess.

Befuddled, Dorothy gave the stranger a quick look, then said, "Come on! We need to catch her!" She did not wait to see if he followed, but was pleased all the same when she heard his footsteps behind her.

By the time Dorothy reached the hallway beyond the Princess' chambers, though, their quarry had vanished from sight. Toto was quick enough, the girl knew, but he would not have expected the Princess to have outdistanced them all so quickly.

In a moment, Toto appeared from around a corner in the hall and trotted towards the man and girl standing by Ozma's chambers. The dog gave a quick, gruff bark as he approached, clearly not happy with what had just happened.

"Where's Ozma?" asked Dorothy when Toto reached her side. "Or whoever that was, 'cause I know it couldn't have really been her."

"It was Mombi," said the young man again. "She took Ozma's place with magic and was running the palace."

"Mombi was here?" asked Dorothy, aghast. The fact that she had already been told this had escaped her for the moment. "For how long? And where's Ozma?"

Toto snorted derisively, then led Dorothy and the young man back into the Princess' room. He quickly made his way to a large green emerald that lay discarded on the floor, and lowered his head. "This is her," he said simply.

Dorothy rushed over to the gem and knelt down to take it into her lap. "Are you sure, Toto?"

Toto only whined in response.

The Kansas girl quickly looked around the room. "The Belt, Toto. With the Magic Belt, we can change her back!"

The small dog rushed over to where the ruins of the once elegant dresser was and could be heard pushing aside pieces of wood searching for the belt. Wasting no time, he dragged the large object to his longtime companion and yipped when it was within arm's length.

Dorothy turned away from staring into the facets of the gem – could she see her Princess' face deep inside the gem, or was that her imagination? Taking the Belt in hand, she wiped at tears streaming down her face and laid lay the belt higher upon her lap. She did not have any desire to put down the gemstone in order to fasten it to her waist this time.

Dorothy scrunched her eyes and tweaked her toes, trying to pull upon the will needed to use the belt. "Change Ozma back," she whispered.

In an instant, it happened. One moment, the strangely warm emerald was in Dorothy's lap, and in the next, a blond curly head was there instead. Ozma's magnificent smile radiated from her face as she raised a hand to lay across the side of Dorothy's own.

"I am safe now, Dorothy," said the Princess. "Thanks to you, I am safe once again."

Chapter 12

Fenstel's Story

Alice squinted her eye against the green glow. It somehow made her queasy to look at, but she dared not look away for fear of missing some critical detail.

From below, the tall girl could hear whispered anxiety in the voices of her friends as some kind of argument ensued. She tried to focus past what was going on below though. Nick Chopper was the one in danger, after all.

"How did you..." started Chopper, his hand raised to his brow to block out some of the light. "If you could--"

"That's not Alasia," called Alice, sensing Nick's confusion. The girl moved back and leveled her hand to the window sill, readying herself if the Tin Woodsman needed her help.

"I see you there, Wyrd girl," called Fenstel. "Just as I know of the others below. There will be no surprises this day but my own." As she spoke, the light on the broom's bristles flared and now there was genuine green flame surrounding them. The witch lowered the broom towards Nick. "Make one wrong move, and I shall melt our fair tin man into so much slag before you can get your hand through that window!"

Alice halted her gesture. It was true, she would have reached in, but could she make it fast enough to save the Tin Woodsman? Doubt made her hesitate, and the hesitation led to indecision, which was precisely what Fenstel had hoped for apparently.

"Now," said the former Wicked Witch of the West, "I can smell Alasia below, so I know she is with you. I would speak with my sister witch now."

"Why?" asked Alice, as she could not think of anything else to say.

"Because my sister is the one witch who cannot lie," answered Fenstel. "And I would know the truth of things."

"That hardly seems an answer," retorted Alice. "In fact, that would be much like me saying that the sky is blue because it is not raining." Alice thought the response quite educated, but she also knew that she was at best only buying time. She quickly looked below, but in the darkness, she could not make out who was who moving around in the shadow of the castle.

"Do not try my patience, girl!" spat the witch inside the castle. "Bring me my sister witch, or watch your tin man melt!"

Alice hesitated a moment, looking again downward before she answered. "Will you promise not to hurt Nick Chopper if I go to talk to Alasia and the others? For I am sure they cannot hear all that is going on from down there."

Fenstel visibly considered the request, a sly grin twisting the side of her mouth. "Only if you do not take so long as I get bored," she laughed. "My curiosity of what a melted tin man would look like might win out."

Alice gulped at the answer, then closed her eyes. In a moment, she felt herself falling once more to stand at the height of her companions below.

"Fenstel was waiting for us," blurted Alice the moment she opened her eyes.

"We could tell *that* much," barked Alasia. "The green glow gave it away. It was either Fenstel or Mombi, and we all know Mombi is pretending to be Ozma in the Emerald City."

Alice could just make out Glinda's disapproving frown in the dark. "Is that truly needed?" Turning to the girl from Oxford, she asked, "What does Fenstel want, Alice?"

"To speak with Alasia," responded the girl, nodding towards the old witch. "She says she needs to know the truth of something, and it seems she thinks only Alasia can tell her."

Glinda turned to her fellow witch. "What do you think? None would fault you if you would not wish to stand alone against her."

Alasia spit at the ground before she answered. "That would be about the right of it," she grunted. "When it was only Fenstel and I left in Oz, after Mombi and..." Alasia's eyes darted towards Glinda, "*Theysla*... were defeated, we were the only true Wyrd sisters left. Fenstel was ever seeking advice from me, always fearful of Glinda or Lacosta coming after her next. We did not exactly get along – but we did not war with each other, either. It helped greatly that the Emerald City lay precisely between us so that our kingdoms did not border each other. So having Fenstel come to me for advice? Yes, this does sound like the Wyrd of old.

"That being said," added the old witch, raising a finger to emphasize her point, "Fenstel has been gone from Oz as long as I. Much has changed in that time, and even more than I could have imagined if Fenstel could have been brought into another scheme of Mombi's. Of all of us, Mombi would be the least trusted. So the fact that Fenstel has allied herself with Mombi gives me pause."

All fell silent for a moment, waiting for the witch to continue. It was Betsy who broke the silence. "That is not an answer," she said crisply.

"No, it is not," agreed Glinda.

"Well, it was not intended to be," barked Alasia. "I was only saying what needed saying."

"Alasia," spoke up Alice, "Nick Chopper is being held by Fenstel upon your good grace. If you do not speak with her, she has said she will... melt our friend."

Alasia laughed. "Well, that's always been a risk--" The witch stopped suddenly as Hank kicked her hard from behind. Immediately, she found herself being bumped solidly from the front by the Sawhorse. Both animals took up a position to the front and back of the witch, forcing her to turn sideways to have any hope of defending herself. In the dark, her hands flickered green for a moment, but quickly faded.

"Alright, I see where this is going," the witch shrugged. "But that wasn't needed. I wasn't going to leave Chopper up there. He's my creation, after all, and it's a personal matter between Fenstel and I for her to threaten to undo him. It doesn't matter whether I care what happens to Chopper or not; it only matters that another witch would try to interfere with my work. Fenstel knew that when she made the threat, and knew I could not let it go without an answer."

The old witch turned to Alice. "I have the magic to move there on my own, but we have rules between us witches, not the first of which is not to use magic to enter another's demesne. So if you would be so kind?"

The Oxford girl looked to Glinda for support, and when the Good Witch nodded, Alice did so as well. She closed her eyes, imagined herself falling upward, and in the barest of moments, she was once again the height of the tower.

This is becoming so much easier, the girl thought in passing. But she did not allow herself to dwell on the thought for long, instead leaning down towards the window to speak to the witch inside.

"Alasia is coming up," said the Oxford girl. The old woman inside said nothing, nor did she lower broom which she still held leveled at the tin man's chest. Alice had to deduce that the information was accepted, and bent down to retrieve the other witch.

Only after Alasia stepped in through the window, did Fenstel lower her broom and return it to the sickly green glow it had first appeared as. The two women who looked almost identical in appearance met each other's glare for nearly a minute before Fenstel took a step back and turned, clearly intending to lead Alasia further into the castle. The former Wicked Witch of the East did not hesitate and fell into step behind her sister witch. In moments, both old women had disappeared from view, leaving the room in shadow once more.

"Quickly," came Nick Chopper's voice in the dark, "while they are gone, lower me down."

Alice though did not think that such a good idea. "My good sir, is it wise to leave two witches alone inside the castle? Would it not be better for me to bring the others up?"

There was a moment's hesitation before the woodsman spoke again. "That would probably be a better idea," he acknowledged. There was clear reluctance in his voice, but under the circumstances, Alice could certainly understand.

The Oxford girl knelt down and retrieved her remaining companions. In spite of her size, she could still only lift one person or creature in each of her hands at a time, so she had to kneel twice to manage. Once all were inside, she reached out to take hold of the sides of the window and reversed her magic, pulling herself in as she shrunk to her normal size.

Glinda had been one of the first two raised, and she had quickly lit a soft white light from the tip of a wand she had produced from somewhere. The light was far softer than the harsh green of the other witch's glow, though it lit the area just as well.

A quick exploration by the Good Witch showed the far edge of the room, where a doorway led out onto a banister overlooking the central column of the tower. When she returned from looking beyond the doorway, the Good Witch explained that a stairwell winded itself downward some distance to the left of the door and she could hear voices to the right. It was plain this was where the two other witches had gone to converse.

The Good Witch was apparently satisfied by what she learned, and suggested that she did not see any urgent need to do more than wait. "Alasia, for her gruffness, has agreed to aid us against Mombi. And as Fenstel has said, Alasia is the one Wicked Witch who has never lied. So if Fenstel seeks to lure Alasia away, I would suspect that at the very least our companion witch would feel the need to stay to her pattern and correct any misconceptions."

"And if they decide to strike out on their own together?" asked Hank gruffly. "What's keeping them from doing that?"

"This *is* a Wicked Witch's castle, Glinda," added Betsy. "If they decide to work together, we are in a bad place to try to stop them, aren't we?"

Glinda's lips pursed for a moment. "Then we will handle that if it happens. The one advantage we have is that this castle is not either of theirs. It's Mombi's. So really the only one who would gain anything by fighting here would be the one Wicked Witch who is not present."

There was some small comfort in Glinda's words, but Alice had thought of another concern, one she chose not to voice immediately. *This may not be their castle, but Fenstel already has Alasia's – what happens if they go there?*

Alice's concerns were shelved regardless, for at that moment, the two nearly identical old women reentered the room. The two looked at each other, and one of them stepped forward.

"We have agreed that I should explain some things," said the woman.

"Fenstel," said Glinda as her only acknowledgment. Alice could only guess at how the Good Witch could tell the two apart.

"As you know, I have been working with Mombi," began the former Wicked Witch of the West. "As Alasia says, not the most likely of partnerships, but I was fooled into believing Mombi changed and sincere in the arrangement she proposed. At first."

"You do not anymore?" asked Glinda guardedly.

Fenstel shook her head. "I do not. Mombi has shown she cannot be trusted, and I have no desire to serve under her. And if she is not stopped, that is precisely where I will be."

The old witch paused a moment, visibly considering what to say next. "I suppose you need to know what has happened and why I agreed to what I did. Some of you must know what happened between Dorothy Gale and I?"

"She melted you, I was told," said Betsy. "With a bucket of water."

"That is true, yes," agreed the old witch. "And it is not. You see, Dorothy Gale threw water on me as I was using my magic. It doused my magic and spread it all over me, making me appear to melt. What it did was change my shape – not exactly melting me, so much as making me turn into something less... solid. I know I told Dorothy as much, but that was because I believed at the time that was what would happen if I got wet.

"My magic was not one that allowed for shape changing. That was Mombi's magic. So I did not know how to undo what had been done. Dorothy threw another bucket of water at me and flushed me out the door. Unable to do anything else, I fled down a drain once I realized how helpless I was."

"Yes, that is how Dorothy described it," agreed Glinda. "And my Great Book described much the same thing, that you became shapeless and ran down a drain nearby. But we all assumed that you had died that day."

"I would have thought as much myself if I had not been aware at all times of what had happened to me," acknowledged Fenstel. "I lived in fear of melting away for so very long, that it never occurred to me that in Oz, I could not die – even from so great an injury. And as I clearly stayed together, I soon realized that I was not melted, just changed. It is difficult to fully explain."

"Then where have you been all this time?" asked Glinda.

"The drains of my castle all drained into the bedrock below, and it was there that I found myself once I stopped falling downward. It was always dark, and damp, and I was miserable for a very long time. I had no way to tell how much time had passed, and more than once I thought I would go mad. I could not raise myself out of the pit I found myself in, as I did not have muscles any longer, and so I stayed there all these years, helpless and alone.

"That was where Mombi found me. I do not know how she did, but one day there was a bright light and Mombi appeared over me. She gave me shape enough so I could speak and tell her what had happened to me, and at the time, she seemed to feel sorry for me. I doubt that now, but after being alone and cold for so long, I did not think to doubt her.

"Mombi told me that she had lost her powers herself for over fifty years, and that she had only recently regained them. She said she had come to my castle to find me, because she knew I could not be dead, and that she had a plan to once again take over Oz. She also told me of the great trick the Wizard had played on us all, and how he actually had no magic after all. But she also told me of how she missed her sisters, and how she wanted those who had hurt us all to pay for what they had done. I was angry and I was resentful, and so I agreed to help Mombi take back Oz."

Fenstel stopped at this and lowered her head. "I am not asking forgiveness, for my feelings on this have not changed. I *hated* Dorothy Gale with every ounce of my being for what she did to me, and I hated more that the Wizard tricked us all for so long. It was because of this I agreed to help Mombi take back Oz and to rule beside her. But I started to see things in how Mombi behaved toward me, and I began to doubt that she had ever genuinely planned to share rule. But I am getting ahead of myself."

The old witch raised her head again defiantly. "Mombi told me that my castle was now guarded by Winkies and that we could not possibly do anything from there, but that Alasia's old castle had been abandoned. She changed me to look like Alasia, giving me back a body and the ability to leave my dark exile and we traveled to Munchkin Country to take the castle for our own.

"There, we found a Munchkin couple sitting under a tree by the front of the castle, and we took them prisoner. Mombi changed the girl into a small shell, then convinced the young man to work for us to guarantee her safety. We had made a plan – if we could get Ozma to send Dorothy up to the old castle to free the girl prisoner, no one would be left behind to protect the Princess herself. Mombi insisted that whenever Dorothy went on one of her adventures, she always brought along whomever was about who could possibly protect the Princess."

"Only it was not Dorothy in the Emerald City," inserted the Good Witch. "It was Alice."

"Quite so," agreed Fenstel. "But that really did not change anything, since Ozma was still alone and Mombi trapped her quite easily. No one even noticed when Mombi took Ozma's shape and began acting like she was really the Princess."

"We have learned that much," Glinda interrupted. "But if all was going so well, why turn on Mombi now?"

Fenstel looked behind her at her sister witch. "Alasia came to the Emerald City and uncovered the plot. But instead of bringing our sister in on it, Mombi turned on her. I saw in that moment that the Mombi who had come to me speaking of sisterhood and being the last of our kind was a sham. She had never wanted to overthrow Ozma for her sisters – she wanted Oz for herself."

The old witch scowled. "It also occurred to me that my very existence was based solely upon Mombi's whim. It is her magic giving me this shape, and she could take it from me in a moment. I could never hope to challenge her, and I believe that has been her plan all along."

"Isn't there something more?" asked Alasia, stepping forward. The original Wicked Witch of the West shirked at the intrusion, but bobbed her head all the same.

"I also spoke to... Dorothy Gale," admitted Fenstel grudgingly. A collective gasp issued from both Glinda and Betsy at this. "Through one of my mirrors. It seems she found one I had thought lost a long, long time ago. And I have made a deal with her. If she but brings it to me, I have promised to help her. And that must mean that I must also help all of you."

Glinda's face turned pale, drawing Alice's attention. The Oxford girl stepped to the Good Witch's side and asked, "Glinda, are you not well?"

Glinda reached out her hand to Alice in assurance, then turned to Fenstel. "Where... Where did she find an old mirror of yours? Dorothy is not even in Oz."

"No, she could not have been to find it," agreed Fenstel. "For it was left in my original castle, the one I left behind when we all fled the Land."

Alice could see Glinda almost stumble at the mention of this. Something was clearly making the Good Witch unsettled, but she could not for the life of her figure out what it could be. None of the others seemed affected nor even appeared to take notice.

"So... Dorothy is in the Land? Where you came from?" managed Glinda.

Alice changed her earlier observation as she looked to the two Wicked Witches. Though none of her companions had noticed, it was now more than plain that the other two witches had noticed Glinda's discomfort.

"You know," said Alasia, trying to appear casual in how she said it, "with two former Wyrds united, we stand a better chance of defeating Mombi."

"Yes," agreed Fenstel, stepping forward as well. "But not as well a chance as we would have if there were *three* of us again."

"Why would Mombi ever help you defeat herself?" scoffed Nick Chopper, rapping the side of his head. "I may only be made of metal, but even I see that as an impossible plan."

"Not Mombi," purred Alasia. "There were originally four of us."

"Yes," repeated Fenstel. "Four. There were four Witches. Mombi was of the North, I was of the East and Alasia was of the West."

"And our sister Theysla ruled the South," finished Alasia.

By now, both older witches were standing directly in front of the younger witch, and Glinda was made visibly uncomfortable by their proximity.

"Please tell us, *Glinda*," urged Fenstel. "Whatever *did* happen to Theysla?"

"I--" Glinda's mouth moved, but no further words came out.

"Sister, we can no longer afford this secret," said Alasia, resting a hand on Glinda's arm. "We have kept it – all of us have, even Mombi – but if we are to stop her, it must be told. Tell us the truth."

"Yes, the truth," insisted Fenstel, resting her own hand upon Glinda's other arm. "The *truth* of what happened to *Theysla*."

Glinda suddenly screamed, pulling her arms away from the other witches to grab the sides of her head. Her eyes clamped shut and she fell to her knees. Alice tried to go to her, but Fenstel stepped between them. "Not now, Wyrd girl," said the old woman. "This needs doing."

Alasia knelt down and raised Glinda's face in the palm of her hands. "You know, don't you? You've hidden from it all this time, but you *do* know, don't you?"

Tears streamed from the corners of Glinda's eyes. At first she tried to shake her head in the negative, but Alasia would not release her grip. Then abruptly, the Good Witch's eyes shot open and she drew in a sharp breath.

"I know," said Glinda, turning away from Alasia to take in the rest of her companions. This time, the old witch did not resist. "I remember now."

Slowly, Glinda raised herself up, her shoulders drooped lower than Alice had ever seen them. "It's me. I'm Theysla. I am the Wicked Witch of the South."

Chapter 13

Glinda's Secret

"I am Theysla," repeated Glinda, rolling the sound around in her mouth, tasting the truth of it yet still disbelieving it herself. "Or at least... I was."

Looking around, the Good Witch could not help but notice that most of her companions were stepping back, distancing themselves from the one person they had all known and trusted through the years. Her own words were condemning her in their minds. There was just so much they did not know, and she was not convinced that they were mistaken to pass judgment on her. At least not yet.

It was not all there yet for Glinda, either. The acceptance that she had been the Wicked Witch of the South was there, the truth of it at any rate. But the details – the facts of how she had changed, were absent still.

The younger witch looked to the two older ones – her sisters from a former life, a past existence that was revealing itself to her piece by agonizing piece. She was so much younger than they were, but if she had been Theysla, that should not be, either. What *was* the truth of all this?

Fenstel came up to the Good Witch and planted herself directly in front of her. The former Wicked Witch of the West squinted one eye – likely the one that did not actually exist in her real body – in order to concentrate on Glinda's face. "She still does not have it yet," the old witch said, clearly speaking to the other elder witch in the room. "I can see the confusion in her eyes. Theysla is still too far away, buried too deeply."

"Are you sure she's even in there?" asked Alasia.

Fenstel ground her jaw as though chewing on a piece of cud, then smirked. "Perhaps not all of her, but there's enough there, I think, to be what we need."

"Wait just a minute," spoke up Betsy. Glinda turned her eyes to look upon Dorothy's old-time companion. Of all her friends, Betsy and Alice alone had been the ones to not step back uncomfortably. Now, Dorothy's friend took a step towards the three witches. "How can Glinda possibly be this old Witch of the South? That's not even possible. She looks nothing like either of you."

"First of all," responded Alasia, "Fenstel and I only look like each other because Mombi made her look like me. This is not how she looked before Dorothy Gale doused her with water. But more importantly, Glinda does not look like herself, either. When she became Glinda the Good, she changed herself physically to make herself appear younger."

"Why would she do that?" scoffed Betsy.

"How should I know?" Alasia shrugged visibly. "And why should we care? How she looks doesn't change anything."

"Except," offered Alice, "you have said only Mombi could disguise people."

Alasia opened her mouth to retort, then slammed it shut. The old Witch of the East turned to her elder lookalike. "That's actually a good point. I'm surprised we didn't think of that before."

Fenstel opened her right eye wider. "Yes, yes," mumbled the former Witch of the West. "How *did* you change without Mombi's help?"

Glinda's mind raced with images, disconnected memories that did not seem to have any connection to anything she had ever experienced before. It was from this miasma of chaotic thoughts that she had drawn the knowledge that she had actually been Theysla, but the thought was completely disconnected from any of the others. There seemed no order nor structure to the images flashing through her mind, and it made her head hurt.

"I have no idea that I even did," said Glinda, closing her eyes and resting her face in her hands. "I'm not even sure that what I said before is right..."

"Oh, it's right," said Fenstel. "We've known it all along. Why did you think the remaining witches did not move against you when you 'defeated' Theysla, as you insisted on telling everyone? Did you think that all three of us together could not have retaliated?"

Glinda lowered her hands to look past her fingertips. "I never thought you would leave your own countries," she offered weakly.

Alasia scoffed. "Hardly. We left our countries whenever it was convenient before. But you were a fellow Wyrd, and we had made a pact with you. Our own individual powers relied on trusting each other, and none of us would act against another for fear of making war with all of us."

"At first," added Fenstel, "we thought it all a farce on your part. Some new scheme of some sort. Pretending to be a good witch. Not that any of us understood your reason for doing that, but you were always one who enjoyed manipulating people--"

"Not manipulating!" snapped Glinda. *Where had* that *come from?* Glinda was never cross, but the accusation had for some reason upset her.

Fenstel made a visible production of rolling her eyes, even though she kept her left eyelid closed. "Yes, yes. Always with the words with you." Fenstel lowered her gaze to once more meet Glinda's. "Your talent lay in convincing people of things that were not always as they saw them. So when you chose to pretend to be a good witch, we all thought it something along those lines. I thought you were trying to find a way to sneak in to confront the Wizard, myself."

"It was not until much later that we came to understand that you genuinely thought yourself another person," said Alasia. "And by then, you had gained the Wizard's trust and become an ally of the Emerald City. None of us yet knew of the Wizard's deceits, so we had no choice but to accept what you had done, whatever that was."

"We've kept silent all these years," said Fenstel. "You stayed in the Quadling Country and never acted against us, so we had no reason to do otherwise."

"Actually," put in Alasia, "Mombi and I wanted to expose you. But Fenstel convinced us not to."

"Well, that much is true," agreed the former Witch of the West. "You were the only Wyrd older than I, and I could not let our younger sisters do anything to hurt you. And besides," at this, Fenstel lowered her eyes, "of all of us, you were the one most hurt by what we had done to escape the Land. If this new person you had become gave you some comfort in forgetting, who was I to help undo it?"

"Hurt?" asked Glinda, a familiarity in Fenstel's words ringing true to her. She lowered her hands the rest of the way, focusing on what the other witch had said. "Yes, Theysla was the oldest. And she had been in the Land the longest. She... *I* couldn't accept what we had done to escape. I remember that much..."

Fenstel inched forward, the tip of her nose a bare fraction of space from Glinda's own. "Yes? I see it... Something is there. Focus on that."

The Good Witch of the South tried to do as Fenstel said, but she could not precisely pin the memory. As she struggled, the elder witch took her hand in her own. "Speak of it. Don't try to think on it. Telling us brought it up, but thinking about it is driving it away."

"Your eye?" asked Glinda, suddenly gaining an insight into what Fenstel was doing. "You are using your eye to see my memories?"

"Not your memories precisely," admitted Fenstel. "But our sister, yes. I can see her trying to come forward."

Glinda pulled away. "If I stopped being Theysla, maybe there was a good reason."

"Good reason or bad," Alasia spat, "it's bad for us now."

"We *need* Theysla," insisted Fenstel. "I am not strong enough to stand against Mombi. She can undo my body with a thought. And Alasia by herself is not enough. We *need* you to remember who you are!"

"Has anyone considered," put in Betsy, "that if Mombi is pretending to be Ozma, that she also has all of the palace's magic? Including the Magic Belt and the Magic Picture? She could be spying on us even now!"

"The Picture is broken," offered Glinda. "But the Belt... The Magic Belt *is* something to worry about."

Then one of Glinda's jumbled thoughts became clearer. "Or is it?"

"What?" asked the two elder witches in sync.

"Wyrd magic is not the same as faery magic," explained Glinda, not entirely certain where the knowledge came from. "It is why we needed to ground ourselves here, to each build our own castles like we had in the Land. We could not use this land's magic. We had to have our own. And the Magic Belt does not even come *from* Oz – it was actually something the Nome King had in his kingdom and brought here. If Mombi were to try to use the Magic Belt..."

Fenstel cackled in laughter. "It would disrupt her own magic. I see now." To this last, she tapped a finger to her magical eye. "I wonder if she understands that?"

"I doubt it," said Glinda, smiling softly. "Mombi has never been one to think things through."

The Good Witch's eyes flashed open. *That was not her memory.* And from the way Fenstel's own eyebrow shot up, the other witch knew it as well.

"I..." Glinda stopped, then started again. "I think... I was upset. Hurting, as you said. I could not bear the guilt of what we had done. We each had our ties to the Land severed based on our time there. Mombi's was the last of us, so she was able to step away from the Land first. I saw her step into the air and fade away, and each of you followed. But I was last. And I saw it. I *saw* what was happening."

Tears began to flow down Glinda's cheeks anew. "The Land was falling apart. Large pieces were shattering and disappearing all around me. I can only guess at what happened once I left. But I remember... I remember thinking of all the people who *lived* in the Land, about how we had just killed them all. Just so us four could escape, we had destroyed every other living soul we had left behind."

"Yet you did not," spoke up Alice. "For I was in Wonderland. I have seen that people are still there. Well, not people in the most absolute sense, to be sure. For there were rabbits and weasels and pigs and playing cards and other things that were not really people *acting* like they were. But they were very much alive."

A small smile touched the edges of Glinda's mouth. "I am grateful to know that now, but I did not know it then. My innocence, the little girl I had once been, could not accept the deaths of so many for our own selfish desires. For years, I struggled with this battle inside myself – trying to work as the other Wyrds were doing, bending the wills of the Quadlings to my own. But for all my efforts to move forward, I could not cast out my guilt.

"Until one day, I did."

Glinda felt a conviction building within her, a new confidence replacing the doubt that had emerged to confuse her. "In Oz, as we have often said, magic is different. And here, the parts of myself that could not abide one another – the guilt held by my younger self and the selfishness of the older woman I had become – came to be so incapable of existing together, that they came apart. I quite literally came apart at the seams."

Glinda could see the evident shock and surprise in the faces of the two Wicked Witches in the room. A look at her companions showed they were all held as though ensorceled by her words. And perhaps there was something of her old magic holding them enthralled in telling her story. In fact, she was certain of it.

"Do not mistake me," continued Glinda. "I wanted it. I did not wish to be a part of the darker part of myself anymore than I did the more innocent part. And it was no accident, either. It was deliberate. I wanted to be done with my guilt, and it was this part of me that I tried to push out and destroy. So when the conflict became too great for my body to contain, I used my magic to convince *myself* that we could not exist together, and I split in two – the darker, evil side facing in physical form the younger, innocent side. And so great was our inability to abide the other, that we warred.

"We fought for days. We were equal in most things – my darker half more brutal, but my softer side more determined. In the end, my lighter side prevailed and I dispelled the dark side of who I was. And Theysla, the Wicked Witch of the South, was defeated."

Glinda spread her arms wide, encompassing all that she was. "This was the form my innocence took when I expelled my guilt and innocence from my body. I did not change so much as my younger, more innocent self is the shape this part of me took. When I prevailed over my darker self, this was the body that remained."

"So where did the name Glinda come from?" asked Fenstel.

"I could not remember *being* Theysla," explained Glinda. "My mind could not grasp what I had been, perhaps. But I could remember being good and fighting the Wicked Witch of the South. Just nothing before that. So I created the name Glinda and moved away from the jungle where my castle had been, perhaps to distance myself from what I had been. I cannot say for certain. I did not truly have any ambitions at first. I built a new home, one built from white marble and decorated with rubies that the Quadlings brought me in gratitude for defeating the Wicked Witch. They saw me as the Good Witch Glinda, and so that is who I became.

"But you must understand. I genuinely *believed* I was and had always been Glinda. I could remember being no one else once the darker part of myself was dispelled. I never meant to fool anyone. I was Glinda the Good."

"But what of Theysla?" asked Alasia. "What of our Wyrd sister whom we need to fight Mombi?"

"She is inside me, in part," admitted Glinda. "But only in part. I meant it when I said I had dispelled the darker part of myself. So any thoughts or memories that were of darker deeds, including I would imagine the magic of manipulation, is gone, vanquished with the darker part of my being."

"Wait a moment," offered Betsy. "I thought people could not die in Oz?"

"They cannot," confirmed Glinda. "But the dark part of me that was Theysla was never truly alive. She was only half of a life, so when she was defeated, she did cease to exist."

Betsy shook her head and crossed her arms. "I'm not buying that," said the girl. "If that were true, you would have only been half a life and ceased to exist, as well."

"You don't..." Glinda paused in what she was going to say, her brow furled.

When the Good Witch said nothing more, Betsy pressed home her point. "How do we know that the darker half of yourself is not somehow still alive, hiding somewhere in Quadling Country? Or maybe even outside of Oz itself? After all, everyone believed that both the Wicked Witches of the East and West were dead, but both have proven to be able to live in secret all this time. Why not the Wicked Witch of the South, as well?"

Glinda felt a chill pass through her at the thought. "I had not considered that before," she confessed.

"Fenstel?" came a sudden voice in the room. Glinda's heart leaped as she recognized its owner instantly, all thoughts of her now restored history shelved for much brighter news. "Fenstel, are you there?"

The former Witch of the West reached into her robe and produced a small mirror, which emitted a green glow so common to the witch's magic. "Dorothy Gale?" asked the witch of the glass. "How is it you have Mombi's glass?"

"Mombi's...?" Glinda grasped the meaning immediately – Dorothy was once again in Oz!

"Mombi is gone now," came Dorothy's voice. "She was disguised as Ozma, but Toto and I beat her. She escaped and we've rescued Ozma! I found this mirror in Ozma's room and guessed it was one of yours."

Fenstel looked up at those standing around her. "It would seem our purpose for gathering is no longer needed, after all," she said, menace creeping into her tone.

"But I gave you my word," continued Dorothy's voice. "I have your mirror. The one from the Looking Glass World."

A sneer spread across the old witch's face. "You don't say." Fenstel was visibly hard pressed not to giggle in what she said. Glinda felt something building, saw Alasia take a step back. Even her other companions tensed at realizing that whatever peace had existed between them was coming to an end.

"I will need that mirror soon, girl," purred the Witch of the West. "But I think perhaps it would be unwise to come to the Emerald City to retrieve it."

Dorothy could be heard speaking with others in the background before she continued. "I can come to wherever you are. We have the Magic Belt."

Glinda allowed herself a small internal sigh of relief at that news, knowing that Mombi did not have access to possibly the most powerful relic in Oz. But it did little to quell her fear of what was coming.

"Dorothy," called out the Good Witch.

"Glinda?" came back the Kansas girl's voice. "Is that you?"

Fenstel held up her hand menacingly, the sickly green glow of magic surrounding it. "She is here, Dorothy, but I am about to leave. Meet me in the one place in all of Oz where we share history. You'll know it is the only safe place where we could meet."

The former Witch of the West wasted not another moment, damping the mirror's glow. Glinda's wand sparked, but Fenstel had already raced across the room. Within two steps, she had straddled her broom and in the next, she was airborne, flying out the window and into the darkness of the night.

"That was quite rude," commented Alice.

"What was that all about?" asked Betsy.

"Nothing good," said Glinda, looking towards Alasia to see whether the other witch were planning anything.

"Don't look at me that way," scowled Alasia. "This isn't any of my doing. But what was that girl saying about Fenstel's mirror from a 'Looking Glass World'?"

"I cannot begin to imagine," admitted Glinda. "But I think we had best make haste to the Emerald City without delay. For I have a dreadful fear that Dorothy is about to give Fenstel something that will be worse for Oz than anything that Mombi had planned."

Chapter 14

Wyrd Deception

"I do not like this, Dorothy," said Ozma. The royal princess sat on the edge of her bed, her posture betraying no sign of any recent trauma. Dorothy had watched this girl for decades, yet she had never been more impressed with her dearest friend's personal strength than she was at this moment.

"Ozma, I made a bargain," explained the Kansas girl for the third time. As she spoke, Dorothy transferred the contents of her satchel to a dark green felt bag which the Princess had provided. She had already stored Fenstel's old mirror, and she now packed a few other smaller items which she felt she might need on her latest quest. "Fenstel gave me the secret of using her mirrors, and I cannot believe she would have done that if she were not trying to be fair. I know who she is, and I know what she's done before. But without her help, I could not have spoken with the Wizard. And I would not have been where I needed to be for the Magic Picture to find me when Toto needed to bring me back here to save you."

"And all she wants is some old broken mirror from her time before she came to Oz?" asked Ozma. "Do you truly believe that is all she wants from you? You *did* melt her, and this all started over a threat to destroy Ozmandia if you were not brought to her. True, we were told it was the Wicked Witch of the East making the request, but now that we really know who was there--"

Dorothy put down the bag and knelt in front of Ozma, taking the Princess' hands in her own. "I know. You have already told me all of this. And I know Glinda and Alice are out there somewhere as well. But since Fenstel was just with Glinda, I have to believe my best hope of finding all that has happened while you were Mombi's prisoner is still with *this* witch.

"And besides," added Dorothy as she regained her feet. "You will have the Magic Picture to watch over me, and the Magic Belt to call me back if Fenstel tries to harm me. That is more than you normally have when I go on an adventure."

Dorothy smiled and her grin infected the Princess' features, as well. "I know. This all should be very simple. But if it's not--"

"Ozma, I need to do this," interrupted the Kansas girl. "I gave my word. If nothing else matters, that much does. It's what keeps people like us from becoming wicked like the witches – we always do the right thing." Dorothy's smile beamed all the more. "I love you for caring, Ozma, but you know I'm right."

The royal princess sighed. "I do."

Dorothy retrieved her bag, then lifted the Magic Belt from where it lay beside the Princess and laid it in her lap. "Then please wish me to the castle of the Wicked Witch of the West. For that is the only place in all of Oz where we both share a history."

Ozma's smile became wistful as she reached around and fastened the belt to her waist. Giving her closest friend one last soulful, longing look, she uttered the words needed. "I wish Dorothy Gale sent to the castle of the former Wicked Witch of the West."

There was no time for Dorothy to say any further farewells, for she found herself instantly standing on the doorstep to one of the two castles in Oz. She knew of course that there had once been four, but she had only personally known of the two – the one in the east, and this one, the former seat of power for the Wicked Witch of the West. At one point, she and her friends had been held captive here while the witch had tried to steal her Silver Shoes. It had only been her spiteful lashing out by throwing a bucket of water at her captor that had unwittingly undone the witch and freed herself and her fellow captives. And now she was returned to this place, to meet with the most unlikely of cohorts.

Looking about, Dorothy could see two young soldiers walking toward her, dressed in the familiar yellow livery of the Winkie Army. There was certainly no doubt where she had ended up, with the yellow color predominant in everything all around her, but the guards fast approaching confirmed that she was indeed in the right place. She knew that even though Nick Chopper had abandoned the old castle in favor of his Tin Palace, that he kept guards around the old structure. Nick was not one to trust that someone might not want to use the castle for something sinister.

"It might not be a good idea to come closer," called the girl. "I am Dorothy Gale, Princess of Oz, and I am set to meet a very dangerous person."

The two soldiers stopped in their approach and turned to each other. Of course, Dorothy was well know throughout Oz, so her word would not be questioned. But there was obviously something else that made them pause.

One of the men called out, "Princess, you are known to be a fast friend of our Emperor. He has been missing for many days, and we wonder whether you would have word of him?"

This was the first Dorothy had heard that Nick Chopper was missing. She had actually been almost hoping that she could have sent these soldiers after her old friend. The fact that he was missing did more than remove that possibility – it also suggested that there was more of a reason why the former Wicked Witch had requested their meeting be here. If she also knew that the Tin Woodsman was missing, she might have plans to bargain for something from the Winkies while she was here, as well.

"I fear I have not heard from Nick Chopper in some time myself," admitted the Kansas girl. "When I finish here, I will be certain to help search for him. But for now, I do really think you should go away from here for now."

Both men looked at each other and spoke softly between themselves. Then they in turn faced Dorothy, each gave a deep bow, then walked back in the direction they had come. Within a few minutes, they had passed completely out of sight.

The girl took in her surroundings, searching for where the old witch might have had in mind for their meeting. To be honest, she had thought Fenstel would be here waiting for her. Instead, there was only the barren land stretching between herself and the entryway to the castle. Briefly, she considered whether the witch's intent had been for the two to meet somewhere within the castle, but memory of something Glinda had once told her gave her pause.

The Wicked Witches would never abide someone entering their homes without their consent, and so anyone wishing to see a witch would need to wait without until the witch agreed to admit them.

It was part of a story Glinda had told the girl when she was much younger, something about the witch who had once ruled over the eastern Munchkin Country, but it held true here, as well. Though the witch who named herself Fenstel might not live within the castle any longer, it could be seen as an insult to wait within. And so Dorothy remained without.

It had barely been dawn when Dorothy had been transported to Winkie Country. And the witch was certainly not in any great hurry to appear. After an hour waiting, the girl reached into her bag to pull out Mombi's mirror that she had found beside Ozma's bed. Moving her hand along the mirror's edge, she awoke the magic and called out to the witch.

"I am here, Fenstel," said Dorothy. "In front of your old castle. Am I in the right place?"

The witch's face did not appear in the glass as it had before, but an ominous green glow rose from the glass as a voice resonated from within. "Yes, Dearie, you are in the right place. But I do not have the advantage of moving there instantly. It still takes me some time to reach places I wish to go. I am flying there as we speak."

"Do you have any idea of how long?"

"Be patient, girl," came the voice. "It is a small thing I ask. I shall be there soon." And with that, the glass dimmed and became once again a simple reflecting glass.

Well, her manners have not improved, thought Dorothy.

The girl was about to place the mirror back in her bag when another idea came to her. Once more, she ran her fingers along the edge of the mirror, but this time called out to someone else entirely.

"Wizard, it's Dorothy. Can you hear me?"

In a moment, the glass shimmered green, then parted to show the Wizard standing in the old castle library where the girl had last seen him. "Dorothy, I had thought you would be here by now. Is everything alright? Did you escape the Looking Glass World?"

"Yes, and I am sorry I did not think to tell you sooner." Dorothy did a quick mental sort of all that had happened to her so she could relate them to her friend, but quickly decided to skim over the more intricate issues. "I came out of the Looking Glass and into the sitting room, but it took me a really long time to find the garden where the Rabbit's Hole was. But just as I found it, I was called back to Oz by the Magic Belt."

"Then tell Ozma to send you back! I need Mombi's book--"

"Wizard, there is more," the girl interrupted. "Mombi was there. She had captured Ozma and turned her into an emerald. Toto was the one who brought me back, and Mombi was disguised as Ozma."

The Wizard's face registered the shock of the news. "Is the Princess alright? Do you have Mombi now?"

"Mombi escaped. Toto has said she turned into a blackbird and flew away. But there is so much more going on here now, that I could not come directly there. I am waiting now to meet with Fenstel--"

"Fenstel?!" demanded the Wizard. "You should not be meeting with her, Dorothy. Not before this Wonderland business is taken care of."

"Wizard, there are things here that are *just* as important. Mombi is loose, and Fenstel was working with her. Now Nick Chopper is missing, and Alice of Oxford is wandering around somewhere in Oz with Glinda. And none of us know what Mombi's plans are – except for Fenstel. I *need* to meet with her, and then I can have Ozma send me back--"

"Dorothy, please tell me someone else is with you."

"No, but--"

"Child, *please* listen to me," interjected the Wizard. "Fenstel cannot be trusted. You need someone there."

"Ozma is watching me, Wizard," insisted Dorothy. "She will call me back with the Magic Belt if anything happens. But this is our one chance to find out what Fenstel knows."

The Wizard was silent for a time, stroking his chin. "Can you keep this mirror enchantment working? While you meet with the witch, I mean?"

"I suppose. As far as I know, it will stay working until I turn it off. That is, Fenstel told me to make certain I turned off the magic when I was done so no one else could spy on me."

"You know," came a disembodied voice, "that does sound like a swell plan."

Dorothy looked up sharply to see a disembodied feline head hanging in the air in front of her.

"Though if I were you, I would hide that away before the witch got here."

"Dorothy, is that...?" asked the Wizard.

"The Cheshire Cat," confirmed Dorothy. "I'm not sure how, but he's here. Or at least his head is."

The cat's paw materialized out of the air without warning. And though it was not physically attached to the feline's head, it began to jab in a direction behind Dorothy. "Ahem," said the cat.

Dorothy turned around to see the silhouette of a figure moving toward her at great speed. It appeared to be a woman sitting in midair, and instantly Dorothy realized who it must be. Quickly, she pushed the mirror into her bag and turned back to thank the cat. However, the cat was no longer anywhere to be seen.

The girl had no time to dwell on that, however. The witch would be there any moment.

"Wizard, if you can hear me," Dorothy whispered, "the witch is here and I can't talk right now."

The former resident of the castle was indeed moving quickly, as she crossed the distance within another minute's time. With delicate ease, she landed upon the ground, pulling free the broom upon which she had been sitting as her feet touched the earth. Without breaking stride, the witch walked over to stand face to face with the girl who had vanquished her once before, the broom held at her side much like the cane she had once used.

"I do hope," said Fenstel, glaring at Dorothy, "that you do not plan to splash me with water again."

The girl gripped the strap of her bag. "Not if you don't try to steal my shoes."

The old woman cackled at the humor. "Those things? Bah! Emerald shoes may be quite pretty, but they hold no magic I would want. Your shoes are quite safe."

The two women fell into silence for a moment, sizing each other up. Dorothy ran her hand down along the side of her bag, feeling the lump that she knew was indeed a flask of water. She had no way of knowing if she would need it, but water had worked against this witch once before. And there was no need to not bring along some kind of insurance.

Finally, Fenstel turned away from the girl and looked up at her castle. "Seen better days, though one would not know it by looking at its walls," glowered the old woman. "But I dread to see what the floors look like after all these years."

"I don't think the Winkies will let you live here anymore," offered Dorothy. "But I am sure Ozma could arrange--"

The elder witch turned on the girl. "If I chose to live here, none could say otherwise," she sneered. "But as I do not intend to, it is a moot point. No, I have other thoughts on the matter.

"Speaking of which, I believe you have something of mine?" Fenstel's right eye gleamed at the mention of what had been brought for her.

Dorothy reached into her bag and felt around, finding the frame that had no glass in it by its feel. She pulled it free, offering it to Fenstel. "It's broken," the girl reiterated. "I told you that."

The witch reached out and took the object reverently. For the barest of moments, Dorothy thought she could sense genuine humanity in the old woman, seeing a sign of nostalgia manifesting in the shaky hands that took back the old mirror.

"It is of little matter," said the old witch. Her hands caressed the old frame, presumably recalling the feel of the antique item with her fingertips. Then, all of a sudden, the frailty passed and the old woman clutched the handle of the mirror in a firmer grasp.

"How much do you know of how my power works, girl?" asked the former Witch of the West.

"I know you can see very far away," said Dorothy. "Other than that, you just had things you used that had magic, like the Golden Cap."

"Partly true," purred the old woman, turning her back to Dorothy and facing her castle. "I can see both with my one eye far and wide, or through any reflected surface that has been enchanted to be seen through. Mirrors work best, for glass is so easily worked with. It is pure and open to being changed.

"Like with this," to which the old woman held the mirror to her side. "It was my childhood toy that I brought with me to the Land, so very, very long ago. I put my magic upon this mirror first, upon both the glass and the metal of the frame. To me, they are one object, even though now the glass of the mirror is in my old castle, and this empty frame here."

Dorothy could sense the dread filling the air moments before she sensed the energy building around the old woman as she continued to speak. "You see, being one thing to me, I can repair what is broken, bring the glass back to be part of the frame – no matter where it is."

Green lightning began to crackle out from the frame in the witch's hand, and she drew it back toward her chest. Soon, the air all around the old woman began to spark with electrical bolts, each strike growing more and more beyond the body of the witch.

"But that is not all, Dearie," said Fenstel, turning back to face Dorothy. "You see, you left the glass in my old castle, and through the bond I have with this mirror, I can now also reach my old castle, as well. And beyond that castle, I can feel the whole of the realm which surrounds it. Wherever the power of my castle is bound, I can now reach out to it – through this small gift you have given me."

Dorothy was forced to shield her eyes and take a step back, so powerful were the bolts of green energy shooting from the witch now. Worse, the energy was beginning to latch onto the ground where it struck rather than retreat, creating tendrils between the witch and the world around her. Behind the witch, Dorothy could also see tendrils reaching as far as the walls of the castle itself. Fenstel was somehow merging herself with the world around her

– and whatever she was doing was only becoming more powerful.

Fenstel's shape shifted and the image that she had worn faded away, to be replaced once more by the familiar image of the one-eyed old woman who had once taken Dorothy hostage, the same old woman whom the girl had defeated with a bucket of water. Desperately, Dorothy fumbled for the flask of water in her bag, but she found herself falling backwards before her hand could find it.

"You still don't understand, do you?" called Fenstel over the roaring crackle of power all about her. "You likely think this is just about me gaining power, but it is so much more! Don't you see? If I can bring the *glass* here through my bond, and I can now touch *all* of the places my old castle's power touches as well as the glass..."

Whatever Fenstel said next was drowned out in a wave of energy greater than before. But Dorothy no longer needed to hear the explanation. She had heard enough to reason it out herself. Fenstel was not just bringing her mirror back, or even the castle – she was bringing the entire Looking Glass World to Oz!

Dorothy looked around her in desperation, watching the natural yellow tint of all things in this country dimming beneath the power of the emerald light.

But if the Looking Glass World is brought here, what will happen to the world that is already *here? What will become of Winkie Country?*

Chapter 15

The Cat's Plan

Oscar Diggs paced around the library in a frenzy. The mirror through which he had been monitoring Dorothy had revealed all: the Wicked Witch of the West was on the verge of destroying Oz, and he was trapped in Wonderland, no closer to a solution of summoning the witches back to their native land than he had been at the start.

The witch's cackles had long since been drowned out by thunder and crashes, and even the mirror itself had begun to show signs of what must have been dominating Winkie Country. Small green arcs of lightning were sparking from the glass, threatening to eventually leap from the frame into this world as well. So far, the sparks of energy fizzled out within an inch of the mirror itself, but with the gathering strength of whatever magic Fenstel was using growing more and more powerful, the Wizard feared that only one of two possibilities remained – either the magic would negate the sole connection he had to Oz, or it would eventually reach out to consume this land, as well.

Clearly, for the sake of this realm, the former was the better solution – and if Oscar knew how to turn off the mirror himself, he might have chosen to do just that. But doing so would have also cut off any hope that Land of Oz might have, even if he had no clue whatsoever how to do anything to help.

Hobbling on his cane, the old man moved from pile to pile of books and papers, uprooting many in his search for something, *anything* that might help. It was pure desperation motivating his actions, for if he had not found any solution in the last several days, he most definitely was not likely to find it in the last possible moment. Yet his very existence since coming to Oz had been ruled by chance circumstances that would somehow ultimately make victory possible, and it was upon this bare chance that the Wizard continued to hope. True, he had never in his life dealt with something that threatened to wipe out an entire realm of existence, but it was all he had to rely on.

After several minutes of rushing about, the Wizard returned to the glass and shouted at it once more. "Dorothy! Dorothy, can you hear me at all? What is happening?!"

Only loud, cacophonous roars and rushing wind answered his pleas. If his longtime friend and companion had even survived at the heart of the devastation that must be happening, she could either not hear him, or was not able to be heard over the chaos herself.

"I don't see why you are so upset," came the now all-too-familiar voice from behind Oscar. The old man turned and was not the least surprised to find the Cheshire Cat sauntering through the rubble of papers on the ground, passively pawing at one particular page that chose to rustle as he walked past. "It is not like it is the end of the world or anything."

"That is *precisely* what it is," barked Oscar, slamming his cane upon the floor for emphasis. "Your witch or wyrd or whatever you call her is destroying Oz!"

"Only part of it," offered the Cat in assurance, plopping suddenly into a small space between several books. The overall effect was of the Cat attempting to nest in the debris on the floor, but the rough edges of the books themselves made it appear to be an entirely uncomfortable position.

"Part of it or all of it, it's still destruction!"

The Cat cocked his head sideways, giving the particular appearance of waiting for something to fall out of his ear. "I suppose," he said absently. Unsatisfied with whatever he had expected to fall out, the cat reached a paw around and batted at it.

Oscar took a deep breath to calm himself. He could feel his heart racing, but he also knew that the Cheshire Cat was likely the only help he might likely have. And to vent his anger upon the Cat at this juncture might cost him whatever assistance the feline could provide.

"Cheshire," the Wizard said as kindly as he could manage, spreading his hands wide. "You were just in Oz. And then you came here. Is there any way you could send me back there?"

The Cat let out a great yawn and rolled sideways. Only for the Cheshire, it was not a roll over another area of ground – instead, the creature's sideways movement sent him at an upward angle into the air. But it also made the edges of his body begin to fade from view, giving his overall image a fuzzy appearance.

"Why would you ever want to do that?" asked the feline, his roll continuing as he moved up some kind of invisible ramp. It seemed the Cat was intent on taking on the appearance of Dorothy's log, Bark, rolling like an over-sized, plush wheel up into the air.

"To help, of course."

"Would it not be easier to help from here?"

"And how would I do that?" asked the Wizard, feeling his patience shredding.

The Cat's head stopped his rolling, ending his ascent some five feet in the air. However, his body continued to move up even further. "Dear Oscar," purred the feline, "have you not been listening?"

The Wizard could think of nothing to say. *Listening to what? To the sounds of my home of fifty-odd years being dismantled through the magic glass?*

When the old man said nothing, the Cat gave an elaborate sigh. "The old girl *told* you what she was doing and *how* she was doing it. Surely if a cat can see the way in, a great and powerful old man can."

The Wizard squinted his eyes. "She said her mirror was in parts, and she was using the parts in her old castle to bring it to her in Oz. How does that help me here? I have no way to send myself to the Looking Glass World. My magic isn't working right here in Wonderland. I could send Dorothy out of this realm, but not myself."

The Cat let out a groan, shaking his head from side to side. "First," the cat's paw appeared in the air in front of his face, one of its digits raised for emphasis, "your magic will not let you leave because you needed to stay here to do what needs doing. I should think that was obvious."

"My magic..." Oscar's eyes flew wide, and he jabbed his own finger at the cat. "You have been blocking my magic!"

The Cheshire rolled his eyes. "You are boring me," he grumped. Returning his eyes to the old man, his second paw appeared out of the air with another digit raised. A glance higher into the room revealed that the cat's body – which had been rolling towards the ceiling – had now also vanished from sight. "Second, the old girl told you that she she could draw her magic from the shard in this Looking Glass World because she had a bond between them."

The Wizard lowered his hand and scrunched his brow. "I do not see the point in--"

The Cheshire interrupted with a loud *Ahem!* At the same time, both of the Cat's extended digits pointed behind the Wizard.

Oscar turned to face the magic mirror, the green energy rippling across its surface. It took him a moment, but then his mind caught onto what the Cat was suggesting. "The mirror here is *linked* to the one Dorothy has. That's why the green lightning is coming out of the mirror – because the same bond that gives Fenstel the ability to draw the Looking Glass World to her *also* links Oz to here through *this* mirror!"

The Wizard turned back to the Cat. "And Fenstel does not know this link is open, does she?"

"I would think not," purred the Cheshire, a broad smile flashing across his face, "since I made sure your girl put it in her bag before my Wyrd could see it. She must, of course, know your friend has it, but not that you were speaking to her through it."

The Wizard's face cracked with a smile of his own. "You planned this. This is all happening as part of some massive plot you have made possible, isn't it?"

"Oh, my dear Oscar," purred the Cat, his paws crossing below his disembodied head. "Cats do not *plan*. That would be ridiculous. A cat *creates* – opportunities, to be precise."

"So keeping me here was an opportunity? For what?"

"To play with, of course," chuckled the Cat.

The old man closed his eyes again to focus. The Cat was helping – but he was not helping in a straight line. It was up to the Wizard to draw the Cheshire back to the proper path.

Opening his eyes, and plastering a show business smile on his face, the Wizard said, "So you created an opportunity. I can see that. But how can I do anything from here, even with a link between Oz and Wonderland? You clearly do not wish me to leave, so whatever you are... *creating*... must be done from here. Can you at least tell me what it is we need to do before it's too late to do anything?" At this last, the old man flung his arm behind him to indicate the crackling mirror.

The Cheshire Cat's eyes closed to slits and for the first time, Oscar could sense genuine menace there. A sinister gleam flashed in the feline's eye as he spoke again. "I created the Wyrds by teaching them my own magic, but I did not *give* it to them outright. I still possess far more than any of them, even working together."

"So you can keep Fenstel from moving the Looking Glass World to Oz?"

"No. I have not been to this shard you call the Looking Glass World. I do not know the path. But your friend Dorothy *has*. She has *some* of my magic in her, but she has far more *faery* magic, which is why I cannot reach through her to connect with my lost shard."

The Wizard was beginning to grasp the Cat's purpose. Yet he also detected the reference to "shards" - something he would need to ask the Cat about before this was through. Just not now. "My magic was taught to me by a faery witch."

The Cat hissed in amusement. "Not at all. You were taught faery magic, but not by a faery *witch*. Which is why you are such a perfect toy – you have influence of both inside you, just as your friend Dorothy has, though in a different way."

The Wizard's brow furled again. "I don't understand--"

The Cheshire's paw batted back and forth in the air. "That part is boring, so I don't care to talk about it. But what does matter is that your magic can be used with my magic to save both the Land and your Oz."

"How?"

The Cat's head floated eerily downward through the air to hover in front of the Wizard. All humor was completely gone from the Cheshire Cat now, a darker, more ominous air dominating his features for the first time. What had been hinted at before had all at once become crystal clear. This was not a mad creature like that Hatter King – this creature was far more sophisticated and intelligent than anyone might first believe. And the true character lying beneath possessed a confidence that only those in absolute control could ever convincingly display.

In that moment, the Wizard of Oz believed he could very easily come to fear the Cheshire Cat.

"By following my directions precisely. I will give you leave to use your magic, but only if you agree to let Fenstel move her lost shard to Oz."

"But you said--"

"The old girl's magic cannot be stopped, Oscar. Not without destroying one or both realms. But there are ways to assure that both survive. We must help the old girl send her shard to Oz, Oscar. But *not* to Winkie Country.

"Surrounding Oz is a great desert, one where none can possibly live. It is so poisonous that any who touch the sand will die. In my explorations of your Oz, I discovered this place and learned much of its nature. Where none can die in Oz itself, its borders are where anyone *will* die if they touch its sands. It is what gives Oz eternal life – by blocking it in on all sides with death."

"You speak of the Deadly Desert," confirmed the Wizard. "Any who touch its sands will turn to sand themselves."

"And this is where you must make certain the Looking Glass World appears. But to do this, we must also bind *this* shard – the one you insist on calling Wonderland. We must bind this realm to Fenstel's magic, and then through Dorothy, link our magic to the other shard. My Wyrd's spell will work, but only in a way she will not foresee."

"But... If you send these shards to the Deadly Desert, they will turn to sand when they touch it."

"Not if you send the desert sands *here* when you do it," objected the Cat, his grin and mirthfulness returning.

"What you describe..." Oscar swallowed. "It is so much more than anything I have ever tried. Even if I could manage to move an entire *world* with my transportation magic, I could not move more than one at the same time, much less send the sands of the Deadly Desert here, as well."

"Oscar," purred the Cat, his face moving within an inch of the old man's, "were you not listening? I shall be working *with* you. All *you* need to do is fix the locations in your mind. Then we will work together to move the realms where they need to be."

Oscar still had significant doubts, but a glance at the mirror and the amount of energy it was casting forth from its frame made up his mind for him. Whether he believed it possible or not, to *not* try was the worse sin.

"I will need a bowl of water," said the Wizard. "Much larger than the one I used to send Dorothy away. I need it to see the places I will be moving."

"Easily done," said the Cheshire. The Cat leaned into the Wizard's face, actually nuzzling the old man's cheek. Oscar instinctively closed his eyes and pulled away. Yet when he reopened them, he found he was no longer in the library.

Instead, he was in some large underground room with a massive pool at its center. He had never seen this room before, though the surrounding walls indicated that they were still in the castle itself. To his side, he found the mirror had also moved with them, and the Cat's full body was now visible floating in the air over the water.

"This is the wellspring," explained the Cat. "Its magic would have been needed for this, anyways. You may use it to draw the image you seek."

The Wizard went to the edge of the pool and dipped his hand inside, willing an image of the castle in Winkie Country to come to him. At once, he found himself witnessing a massive green maelstrom battering at the ground and walls of the castle. He could see Dorothy lying upon the ground, struggling to crawl away and Fenstel herself hovering in the air, the chaotic energy swirling all about her. The sound of the storm echoed through the chamber from the mirror itself, making it all very real.

"Focus on moving the castles themselves," suggested the Cat. Once more, the feline had assumed his commanding personality. "The land to which they are bound will follow in their wake. The pool is large enough that you can see all that we would move."

"I have never summoned more than one image before," disagreed the Wizard.

"Once you bring one image into the water, I can maintain it. Just concentrate and do this quickly."

Oscar released his hold on the image of the Wicked Witch's storm and was startled that it did not fade. Even though he had been forewarned by the Cat, he had still expected it to vanish. He only allowed his surprise to distract him for a moment however, as he summoned an image of the closest area he could recall of the Deadly Desert – the area lining the edge of Winkie Country.

"That will do fine for this castle," said the Cat. "But you will need to bring this shard, this Wonderland, closer to the castle in Oz that has copied *this castle*."

"What?" The Wizard fumbled and was grateful that the Cat had been true to his word in holding onto the image.

"For this to work, the castles must be bound to their opposites," called the Cheshire over the escalating sound. "The area you have chosen works for Fenstel's castle in the Looking Glass World, but Alasia's is too far away."

"This was Alasia's castle?"

"Did I not just tell you that?" asked the Cat, a hint of his mischievous humor seeping through his more serious demeanor. "Summon an image to the east of Oz for this shard, and then one of the castle in the east, as well."

The Wizard did as he was bid, and soon had four images formed in the massive pool.

"Now, the Looking Glass World."

The old man had never seen the outside of the Looking Glass' castle, but he had seen the interior of the library, and so he brought that image to the water. No sooner had it formed though than control of the image was pulled from him as the exterior of the structure surrounded in snow suddenly dominated the water's reflection.

"Needed to have it be more visible," offered the Cat. "And now... Now it is time to move things about. Remember, Oscar, I will be beside you through this all, so do not focus on what cannot be done. Just do it, and let what is impossible just be."

Oscar Diggs swallowed hard against a suddenly dry mouth. He could feel sweat beading on his brow, but he let go of his doubts and did as he was bid. He reached into the water as Glinda had taught him and focused on the Looking Glass' castle – Fenstel's target. Once he felt he had a grasp there, he moved on to the desert to the west of Winkie Country, amazed at how his grasp of Fenstel's Castle remained under his control. He next reached out to Alasia's castle in Oz, followed by the desert sands to the east of Oz. Finally, he focused on his current location in Wonderland, the easiest of his targets.

The Wizard would never again be able to explain how it felt to master so much magic at once. He did not feel powerful precisely – he just felt able to do it all without effort. He knew in the rational portion of his mind that he was stronger in magic than he had ever been in his entire life, but he did not feel energized or actually any different than he might have by picking up a collection of small rocks. He knew this was the Cheshire Cat's magic he was using, but it did not feel at all strange as he had thought it must. In fact, he could not feel the magic he was using at all.

"Move them, Oscar," called the Cat. "Move them now!"

The old man realized that he had let his mind wander and pulled himself back to the task at hand. With a shrug of his newfound capacity – with an effort akin to brushing dust off a tabletop – Oz the Great and Powerful used his magic to move the objects he had taken hold of. A great burst of energy exploded all around him in that moment, but he did not care. He was blinded in what he was doing, but concern had left him. He did not need his mortal senses to guide him now – he only needed his will. And his will was never in doubt as to whether it would be done.

The next Oscar knew, he was picking himself up off the floor. His entire body was soaking wet, and he could see water splashing upon the ground all around him. A glance above him only brought showering rain dropping into his eyes, forcing him to look away again.

It took a full minute for the waters to stop falling, though drips persisted. The Wizard pulled himself once again to his feet. He looked about for his cane, but it was not immediately visible in the dark cavern. The only light in the room was from the large mirror lying on its back next at the rim of the pool. The entire room was soaked, the water of the pool having exploded outward. The Cheshire Cat was nowhere to be seen.

The old man hobbled over and looked into the mirror. In spite of its position, it appeared that he was looking out over a level field on a brightly lit day. The dark shadow of a castle lurked at the edge of the glass, but what immediately drew the Wizard's eye was the face that was centered in the glass.

"Dorothy," sighed the Wizard in relief.

"Wizard, are you alright?" answered the Kansas girl.

"Yes, yes. Are you?"

"Fenstel disappeared," the girl answered. "And so did her magic. I don't know what happened."

"It is a long story," chuckled Oscar, laughing now more to relieve his nerves than from any real humor. "But I believe we might have some new neighbors in Oz."

"New neighbors?"

"I will explain later. For now, I feel a great need to find a place to sit down very soon." Looking to the side, the Wizard spotted his cane lying upon the ground and made a mental note of its location. "But first, I need to get somewhere dry."

The Wizard smiled to Dorothy, then waved farewell. He walked over to retrieve his cane, then set out to find a way out of this soaking wet room.

Several minutes later, the old man had navigated himself out of the underground chamber and through the castle itself to the great entrance. He wasted no time in breaking the doors' seal and stepping out into the sunshine beyond.

Nothing looked changed to his eyes, but he could smell a difference in the wind. There was a familiar smell to the air, one that suggested a dry desert that had not been present before. It was quickly mixing with the more fragrant scents of the surrounding trees, but there was enough of it that the old man could detect it.

The Cheshire Cat had not been wrong. They had moved worlds today. Wonderland and the Looking Glass World were now part of Oz.

Chapter 16

Oz-Wonderland

Nearly a week had passed since the day Fenstel tried and failed to destroy Winkie Country. Yet for all the chaos the former Wicked Witch of the East had attempted to cause, it did not equal that which sprung up in the days that followed.

Two new countries had materialized at opposite ends of Oz – one bordering Munchikin Country and the other along the border of Winkie Country. But these new territories had no comprehension of boundaries or rules as the residents of Oz knew them, leading to massive intrusions into the Land of Oz by all manner of uncouth peoples. Though the people of Oz were well known for their civility and good natures, many citizens of both countries were taxed to the limit of their patience. It was all that Ozma from her seat on the Emerald Throne could manage to avoid a complete breakdown in the order of both realms.

Though smaller incursions happened, by far the most invasive was a large army of living cards led by a large brown rabbit known only as the Hare. His army would move about with no logical rhyme or reason through Munchkin Country, making it impossible for the Royal Army of Oz to follow and confront the military body. Thankfully, in spite of the fact that they called themselves an army, they were not actually attacking anyone – just charging from one place to another. Oftentimes, reports were received that the army would just abruptly change direction, or even stop and run in the opposite direction for no apparent reason.

For Ozma, it had been an incredible test of her diplomatic skills. Not only did she have civil unrest all through the Land of Oz, but she had needed to send envoys into these new countries seeking diplomatic relations with whomever ruled there. In the place which her guest Alice Liddell called Wonderland, there was at least some greater degree of order than the place called only the Looking Glass World. At least in Wonderland, there was a ruling seat in the center of their realms governed over by the Queen and King of Hearts – but in the Looking Glass World, there were two sets of kings and queens moving about without any real clear seat from which they ruled.

Of course, Wonderland was not completely free of confusion, either – though the King and Queen of Hearts seemed the predominant rulers, there were at least three other sets of Kings and Queens rumored to be wandering Wonderland without any clear seats of power. And this was not counting the recently deposed Hatter King or the Hare who ran around calling himself both King and Queen. Thankfully, no one in Wonderland gave any great credence to the latter two, and in spite of the other Kings and Queens, no one seemed to question the King and Queen of Hearts' predominance over their territory. At least, not that Ozma had been able to find.

After almost a week of effort, the Royal Princess had finally managed to at least bring the primary ruling authorities of both kingdoms together in Oz for a summit. The King and Queen of Hearts had already arrived the day before, while the two royal pairs from the Looking Glass World – known only as the Red and White Kings and Queens – were taking a considerably longer time to reach the Emerald City. Ozma had been told that these two were engaged in some kind of progressive style of movement that delayed their paths considerably. For some reason, none could seem to travel in the same direction for very long, and when they could, there would be members of the entourage who could not move as fast as the others. Her royal messengers described it as an entirely uncooperative and disruptive mode of travel.

In spite of this, the dueling pair of royals had been cited passing through the field of poppies earlier that day, and were scheduled to arrive in the Emerald City within the hour.

In preparation of the ultimate arrival of the Red and White Kings and Queens, Ozma had summoned a small group of her most trusted advisers to her chambers to discuss what could be accomplished by this historical meeting between kings, queens and princesses of three different magical realms. Amongst her trusted companions for the meeting were the Wizard Oz, Dorothy Gale, the Wogglebug and Glinda the Good. Professor Wogglebug had been restored along with the rest of the the residents of the Emerald Palace by the Magic Belt, but efforts to undo any other magics of Mombi's had accomplished nothing – including returning the lost Ozmandia. It seemed that wherever Mombi had the lost palace, it lay beyond the power of the Belt.

Also present was the Princess' royal guest, Alice Liddell of Oxford, who had been gracious enough to remain in Oz to lend her expertise in the subject of these two realms to this meeting. There had been some fear that now that Wonderland and the Looking Glass World had been moved through both time and space, that should Alice be returned to her own time in Oxford, England, that she might not be able to be returned. There had also been concern expressed as well that she might already have been cut off from her own place of origin, though Glinda had assured everyone that Alice's unique magic would always return her to Oxford in her proper time.

"What frustrates me the most," said Ozma once all were seated in chairs and made comfortable, "is the lack of real names. All these rulers have are titles – the Queen of Hearts, the Red King, and so on. Do not any of them have real names?"

"But those *are* their real names," suggested Alice. "In as much as they have names at all. When I first visited Wonderland, it was quite vexing for me, as well. But very few people there even have names, it seems – it is almost as if not having a name made one more important there."

"That makes a very strange sort of sense," said the Wizard Oz. "In our world," to which he moved his cane in a circular pattern to include Dorothy and Alice, "one might spend a lifetime trying to gain a title, whether it be by election or hard work. Some, like royals, are born to it, but others must acquire a title. In a place like Wonderland, there is a strange kind of illogic to everything, where simple things are extreme by comparison. With this in mind, it seems a proper progression of the idea of titles being something that *becomes* one's name rather than something that is added to it. One can only assume that if the Looking Glass World follows a similar nature, that the Red and White royals are similarly defined."

"Or perhaps," put in the Wogglebug in his overly proper fashion, "it is a *symptom* of their disease." When several eyes turned to the over-sized insect for clarification, the great bug puffed out its chest and continued. "Being the highly magnified and thoroughly educated creature that I am, I have had the good fortune to commit myself to the study of afflictions of all sorts, many of which manifest in the form of deficiencies and, shall we say, defects."

The Wogglebug seemed content in his answer, but when blank expressions were all that met his pronouncement, he continued once more. "Perhaps, as a symptom of having their world being *broken*, these people have been harmed in such a way that they are no longer whole, and so they are *afflicted* in such a way as they are not capable of recalling anything more than their titles alone."

"That is a genuinely well thought out idea," agreed Ozma, nodding her appreciation to the giant bug. "Though the Wizard makes a good point, as well. Whichever is true, however, I fear none of this removes--"

"Might it not be instead," offered a new voice, "that they are just too full of pride to *admit* that they have any other names?"

As one, the group turned to the sound of the voice, to find a large grey-striped cat curled up upon the emerald cover of Ozma's bed. As he lay in place, the Cat kneaded out with his claws, digging deeply into the velvety material with obvious great pleasure.

"Might I introduce for those who have not yet met him," spoke up the Wizard, "the Cheshire Cat of Wonderland. I was wondering when you would show up again."

Ozma rose from her chair and made an immediate curtsy to the elusive feline. "Sir Cat, you are most welcome in Oz. I have heard much and more of what you have done to save both Oz and the errant lands who now share our borders."

"Do not look to me," said the Cat, making one long stretch with both legs, "for I am only a cat, and cats do not do such things. At best, we watch and I am very good at that myself, if I do say so."

Alice rose from her chair and moved to stand next to Ozma's bed. "You never do say what you mean, but that is the way of cats. I have much experience with them, you see, and I can tell that much about you."

The Cheshire Cat only yawned in response and lay his head down as though to take a nap.

"Since you are here," said the Wizard, standing himself, "I imagine you have come to say something of import, however you protest. Yet before you do, might we ask a couple of questions of you?"

"I am but a cat," returned the Cheshire, his grin spreading across his face mischievously, though he made no effort to open his eyes. "Who am I to stop you from speaking, whether it be a question or otherwise?"

The Wizard turned to Ozma, and the Princess nodded her consent to permit him to ask his questions. The old man turned to the Cat and asked, "I believe the most pressing concern is, what happened to Fenstel? And for that matter, to Alasia? They both disappeared when we finished moving Wonderland and the Looking Glass World to Oz."

"I truly doubt they disappeared," responded the Cat. "More likely, they returned to what they were before they escaped the Land in the first place. Once their respective castles came here, they bonded with the magic they had already created in this land, once again forcing the Wyrds into their roles as guardians once more. I would suspect that they returned to their own castles where they are even now trying to adjust to their old roles again."

"But I was in Alasia's castle, the one that was in Wonderland" insisted the Wizard. "We both were. And I never saw Alasia appear there."

The Chesire Cat snickered. "Did you search all the rooms before you left?"

"Well, no," responded the old man.

"Then how would you know?" laughed the Cheshire.

"So if what you say is true, what was accomplished by all of this? Why create a situation where these two lands would need to be brought to Oz in the first place?"

The Cat took a deep breath and raised his head. His eyes opened, revealing the highly intelligent seriousness which the Wizard had witnessed before. "The Wyrds were never meant to be witches. They were meant to guide the fortune of the Land. But they shattered the Land into shards, destroying the world as we all knew it. Now, two of those shards have been recovered, but in their broken states, they could not exist on their own without their missing parts. Since none know where all the shards went, the only hope either had to continue to exist was if they were bound to a magical realm which was already whole."

"Oz," said the Wizard simply.

"Just so," agreed the Cat. "The Wyrd girls already set the magic in place to make it happen. They created their own foundations in Oz, manifested their own wellsprings in each of their castles centered upon their own magics. This gave the lost shards something to bond with, much like a lodestone might act to draw another such stone to itself. It was truly the only measure that could be taken to save the Land, even if this is only the first step in greater work yet to be done."

"More shards?" asked the Wizard. "How many?"

"At least four," said the cat, raising its paw and extending the four pads of his foot. "Four castles, four shards. That would be my guess. I imagine there may be smaller fragments out there, but I believe they will eventually be drawn in once the four castles are united again."

"Good Cat," interjected Ozma, "though I can appreciate your efforts to save your realms, I must point out to you that Oz might not be the best place to move these worlds to permanently. Already, there is unrest as citizens of your realms cross into Oz, and there are also new concerns towards the safety of Oz as the Deadly Desert which has acted as a natural defense of Oz have been removed to our eastern and western boundaries. Oz has many enemies beyond these shifting sands, not the least of which lie within the Nome Kingdom – which now by all reports can cross readily into Oz through the Looking Glass World."

The Cheshire stood up, stretching his body straight into the air as he did so. "Who said anything about being forever? The shards of the Land are fragile now, but only because they are broken. If the other shards are found and joined with the two presently here, then the Land can exist *without* your Land of Oz to hold the fragments in place. Seems a simple enough solution to me."

"Did it not occur to you," asked Ozma more firmly, "that the citizens of Oz were not your playthings to be given commands?"

The Cheshire Cat lowered his arched back, hissing in laughter. "Never." With that final word, the Cat turned about, and in doing so walked into the air, vanishing from sight.

The Wizard plopped down in his chair with a great sigh. "Well, that seems to be that. To secure the borders of Oz, we have been charged by a precocious feline to track down his other two lost baubles."

"Yet if we can even find these other shards," asked Dorothy, "is there any guarantee that the Cheshire Cat will really move Wonderland away from Oz?"

"He's a cat, Dorothy," pronounced the Wizard. "Of course there's no guarantee. Cats are fickle by nature, and this one moreso than even your own Pink Kitten. But I do not see that we have any choice. If there is to be any hope to secure the borders of Oz, I think we must accept that we must do as the Cheshire Cat wishes and try to find his missing realms, wherever they might be."

Silence fell over the group for a moment. Finally, Ozma spoke up. "Well, it is definitely something we will need to explore, but for now, I think we must move to the Throne Room. If our estimates are true, the Red and White Kings and Queens will likely be arriving by now, and we should be there to greet them."

None disagreed with the Princess' assessment, and so all followed her from her chambers and through the halls of the Emerald Palace. No one spoke as they walked, a truly uncommon practice in these halls, for all were withdrawn in thoughts of their own – some considering what new threats might exist in the search for new faery realms, while two girls were each secretly excited at the prospect of even more adventures. Dorothy and Alice shared a conspiratorial look as they neared the Throne Room, and each knew the thoughts of the other – what a marvelous road they were set to embark upon!

Of course, Alice would have to return to her own world. She had been away from the school now for over a week, and there were certain be many worrying about her. But no matter what the Wizard and Glinda said, the Oxford girl also knew that she still shared a bond with Wonderland. And if it no longer existed in her own time, then she knew she would be able to return to that magical world – even if it now existed in this time and place.

As the small group entered the great Throne Room of Oz, all thoughts turned to the events transpiring around them. The procession from the Looking Glass World was indeed filing into the room, and much ado was being had by the royal party in how they could orderly enter the chamber. Each had brought other royal personages with them, each party consisting of eight members all told, all scrambling for position in the chamber.

At the center of the room where the Emerald Throne throne rose up upon its dais, two other royally dressed personages already waited – the King and Queen of Hearts. The King himself was a diminutive man, while his wife towered over him in both stature and sheer presence of personality. There was no doubt in seeing the pair in who held the true power of the crown between them.

Ozma left her group standing to the side of the room and climbed the stairs to the Emerald Throne. The Wizard alone followed in her wake, prepared to take the position of royal adviser for this special occasion. He would stand behind and to her right in a prearranged stance, while the King and Queen of Hearts would stand to her left.

As the Wizard took his position, Ozma noticed a certain unease in the posture of the King and Queen of Hearts. There was some unspoken tension between them and the Wizard that had been plain from their first arrival, but none would speak of specifically what lay behind it.

Ozma sat patiently on the throne while she waited for the arriving royals from the Looking Glass World to finally fall in place, standing in two solid lines facing each other across the central aisle of the room.

"It would be more helpful, I believe," offered Ozma, "if we were all facing the same direction. And since this is the throne, I would suggest that we all face this direction."

The White and Red garbed figures looked at each other uncertainly, but eventually complied with Ozma's request. The end result was that of the two rows facing the Emerald Throne, with the King and Queen of each color standing in the middle of each line.

"Perhaps it might be easier" said Ozma, "if the Kings and Queens would step forward to the head of your processions? It might be easier to speak with each other if we are not separated by these others?"

The envoys from the Looking Glass World shared glances once again. The Red Queen seemed to speak for them all. "Would you have the moon fall from the sky, as well?"

"Such impudence," cried the Queen of Hearts, stepping forth with a sneer upon her face. "Off with her--" Suddenly, the Queen stopped and her eyes darted to the Wizard. Swallowing, she took a step back beside her husband, and said nothing more.

Ozma hid a smile behind her hand. *And so begins the history of the joined lands of Oz-Wonderland...*

About the Author and Illustrator

Ron Glick (born January 20, 1969) is a community activist, and is presently active in several charitable enterprises. He was born in Plainville, KS. After living in various states, he currently lives in Kalispell, MT. He is the author of The Godslayer Cycle, Chaos Rising and the Oz-Wonderland series, as well as having written several volumes of Ron El's Comic Book Trivia. He is presently working on the second novel of Chaos Rising. He loves contact and welcomes input on his work through his Facebook page at http://facebook.com/godslayercycle and Twitter @Ron_Glick.

Toni Kerr lives with her husband, two dangerously creative children, and a fabulous Australian Shepherd in the Pacific Northwest. She loves exploring the outdoors, illustration/Photoshop, writing fantasy, live music, and is easily distracted by most creative endeavors.